THE
BOOK
OF
LAMAN

BY COMMON CONSENT PRESS is a non-profit publisher dedicated to producing affordable, high-quality books that help define and shape the Latter-day Saint experience. BCC Press publishes books that address all aspects of Mormon life. Our mission includes finding manuscripts that will contribute to the lives of thoughtful Latter-day Saints, mentoring authors and nurturing projects to completion, and distributing important books to the Mormon audience at the lowest possible cost.

THE BOOK OF LAMAN

Mette Harrison

.

For information contact
By Common Consent Press
4062 S. Evelyn Dr.
Salt Lake City, UT 84124-2250

Book design: Andrew Heiss

www.bccpress.org

ISBN-10: 0998605247
ISBN-13: 978-0998605241

10 9 8 7 6 5 4 3 2 1

Dedicated to my wicked brothers:
Mark, Joe, Rob, John, James, and Peter

Foreword

Mette Harrison is one of the best-known Mormon authors currently writing about Mormonism for a national audience. Her Linda Wallheim mystery series (*The Bishop's Wife, His Right Hand, For Time and All Eternities,* and, one hopes, many more to come) has been absolutely groundbreaking. It marks the first time ever that a strong and intelligent Mormon woman (or any other kind of Mormon woman for that matter) has had a starring role in a nationally marketed mystery series. Linda Wallheim is one of the only Mormons that many of Harrison's readers have ever met.

Harrison is not just one of the best-known Mormon writers today. She is also one of the best. Her mystery novels are as well-crafted as they are intellectually satisfying. Linda is a practicing Mormon, but not an unquestioning one. She relates to the Church on her own terms, sustaining her bishop-husband, but not always agreeing with him, or with the institution he represents. Nonetheless, Linda finds beauty and truth in the Church and in the magnificent, broken, wonderful, terrible, frightened, triumphant people who populate her ward. (That these people have an inordinately high murder rate among them is a requirement of the genre and not a commentary on the Gospel.)

All of this is just another way to say that Mette Harrison is a first-rate novelist who recognizes nuances and subtlety in the way that people live and interact with the divine. When a novelist of her caliber decides to write about Mormonism's most sacred text, we, her co-religionists, would do well to listen to what she has to say,

And she has a lot to say.

The central conceit of The Book of Laman—telling the story of 1 Nephi from Laman's perspective—seems like a perfect device for a funny book. Indeed, Bob Lewis used it precisely this way in his satirical 1997 novel, *The Lost Plates of Laman*. Here we see all of the jokes implied the first time we hear that Laman is the narrating the Book of Mormon: the villain becomes the hero, and the hero becomes an insufferable know-it-all, the archaic language is peppered with anachronisms and modern values, and the devotional content of the original text is sacrificed on the twin altars of mocking Mormon weirdness and having a grand time.

But Mette Harrison's Book of Laman is not funny. It does not try to be funny. It doesn't use intentional archaisms to make fun of the Book of Mormon's language; rather, it tells its story in a non-distracting modern style. The characters are not simply reversed. Nephi is sometimes an annoying brat, but he is also a real prophet who sees and speaks for the Lord. Laman is neither a comic book villain nor a long-suffering ironist. He is a flawed human being struggling to live well and usually coming up short. And in some of the book's very best scenes, he is touched unexpectedly by grace and God.

Harrison's characters are the sorts of people who might actually have existed in history. She does not naturalize the miracles in the Book of Mormon—there really are angels and visions and smiting and all the rest—but she humanizes the actors. And this is important, as it corrects for a reading bias that plagues Latter-day Saints. Simply put: we want the Book of Mormon to be history, not fiction, but we expect the people in it to act like characters in a (not very good) novel and not as the kinds of people who have actually ever existed.

Take, for example, the well-known scene in 1 Nephi 3-4 when Nephi and his brothers approach Laban to ask for the brass plates. Hearing this story in Sunday school, one might suppose that it was the most normal thing in the world for some teenagers to show up at an important man's house and say "the city is about to be destroyed, but don't worry, God wants you to give us the most important thing you own so our descendants don't forget how to read. It's OK. Our dad saw it in a dream." What kind of monster would refuse?

Through Laman's eyes (Chapters 10-12) we see just how insane the brothers must have looked to Laban and anyone else paying attention. They showed up without any recognizable claim to an extremely valuable object and simply demanded that Laban surrender it to them. And when he refused, Nephi cut his head off because he had a subjective feeling that this might be a good idea. Was this God's will? Yes, Harrison clearly believes that it was. But that wouldn't have made it all any easier. In many ways, it makes it even more scary, given what it might suggest about God.

Situations like this abound in *The Book of Laman*. Harrison takes great pains to treat all of the characters as actual human beings who interact with an actual God and who must still agonize over their choices, face their weaknesses, conquer their demons, and do their best to reconcile, however imperfectly, their human and divine natures—just like the rest of us.

For centuries great writers have set new narratives within well-known stories. The question, "how would a different character tell the same story?" gave us both Euripides' *Medea* and the Book of Job—and, more recently, the novel *Wide Sargasso Sea*, the Broadway musical *Wicked*, and the perennial stage classic *Rosencrantz and Guildenstern Are Dead*. These works are at once derivative and interpretive, and they have also become classics in their own right that can be read profitably apart from their departure point.

Mette Harrison's *The Book of Laman* is precisely such a book.

Michael Austin
University of Evansville

1

My father Lehi says he has visions, that God speaks to him. He says that the Jews are wicked and they are going to end up being carried off to Babylon until they repent and change their ways. He preaches this day and night. Now.

When I was a kid, do you know what my father preached then?

Drunkenness, adultery, and gluttony.

You wonder why there's a big age gap between me and Lemuel and our younger brothers Nephi and Sam? Well, that's why.

My father left my mother Sariah for six years. She woke up one morning and he was gone. He hadn't come home the night before.

I still remember me asking her where Papa was.

"I'm sure he's out shopping," she said, but I could see the truth in her eyes.

Lemuel asked her where Papa was that night, when she was forced to cook cakes for us from leftover flour and oil that had gone rancid.

"He's telling stories," she said. "You know how good he is at telling stories?"

He was good at telling stories, but the problem was, they were never true. I had already figured that out, but Lemuel hadn't yet.

When Mother asked him to tell one of Lehi's stories, Lemuel went right into it. It was the story about the talking fish's journey riding on a tiger's back until the fish was swallowed by a camel. But the fish could still speak inside the camel, and told the tiger to attack the camel. And the tiger ate the camel, with the fish inside. And still the fish could speak. And so on, the story went.

Lemuel laughed at the story, and he was still giggling even when he went to sleep that night. I could hear him, lying next to him, feeling the wood beneath his feet jiggle.

Mother was weeping that first night. She wept a lot during those years. I'm sure I didn't hear all of it, but I heard plenty.

She prayed, too. I would catch her sometimes when she was in her room. She would kneel on the floor then, and beg God to send our father back to us.

"I want him because I love him, but I need him for his sons. They need his guidance. They need his laughter. They need his love. I see them longing for him every day. I see their pain, and it pains me doubly. Please, you are a father. You have sons. Please send him home."

But that wasn't the only time she prayed. We lived in a much simpler house then. Only five rooms, and we had two servants who did not live in with us, but came during the day. Or at least, we did until Father was gone. Then Mother dismissed the servants and did all the work herself. Somehow, she managed to find food to give us to eat even when I could see nothing in the house.

She would go into the garden, find some weeds and make a tea. Or she would dig up a root and figure out how to cook it. Sometimes she would trade, this for that, or she would clean for others when it was night and she should have been sleeping. She would think we didn't notice she was gone.

She prayed sometimes when she was working in the kitchen or out in the garden. It wasn't always on her knees. She would look to heaven and she would mouth a few words soundlessly. She would weep when she slipped and she would pray while she was unable to stand. She would pray.

And that was when I learned what prayer was and what it won you.

Nothing.

God didn't listen to my mother and He certainly didn't listen to me.

She wouldn't teach me how to pray. I asked her once, but she patted my head and told me that I must wait until my father came home, because a man always teaches his sons how to pray. So I tried to pray as she did, and I got the same result she did.

If God hears prayers, it is only the prayers of his favorites, as far as I can tell. The rest of us, He ignores because we're not important enough to bother.

Once, we were out on the streets, following Mother as she searched for a cheaper source of thread for the shawl she was working on commission. And we saw him there. Father.

He was surrounded by people. He was standing on a boulder, his arms waving around. His eyes were bright and his nose seemed huge. I remember thinking that he looked different from this perspective. I'd never realized my father's nose was so large.

"And then Moses said to Pharaoh—dance!" said Father's hoarse voice. He lifted his arms in the air and started to move his body.

"Come along," said Mother, pulling me away. "Lemuel, this way." She put a hand on Lemuel's face. He hadn't seen Father there, but he would have, if Mother hadn't covered his eyes like that.

I craned my head backward as she dragged me forward. I was surprised she had so much strength. She had her bag to carry her things in, and Lemuel and I were both smaller than we are now, but we didn't weigh nothing and she hadn't eaten more than a few morsels for a long time. She fed us, but she always gave us what she hadn't eaten because we were ravenous and she said she wasn't hungry.

I looked back and saw Father was dancing frantically, though there was not even any music playing. His body looked like he was having a fit of some kind. Did he need a doctor? Was he crazy? Was that why he left us?

"Why didn't you talk to him?" I asked Mother that night, when Lemuel was distracted.

"Who?" said Mother, but I could see by the tenseness of her shoulder muscles that she had not forgotten.

"Father. You saw him there in the street. He was drunk." And more than drunk.

"I didn't see him. I told you, he is away on a journey. For business. When he returns, we will be wealthy. We will have a new house." She had begun this series of stories with Lemuel at night, fanciful imaginings of what we would all do together when Father returned.

"He was dancing. He looked like he'd been bitten by a snake." I wiggled my whole body in the way that I'd seen my father do it. I laughed.

"Don't laugh at your father," said my mother sternly.

She had forgotten that she was pretending that it hadn't been him.

"Everyone else was laughing at him," I pointed out.

"They were laughing with him," said Mother. "He's always been a man who can get a crowd to listen to him. That's his special gift. He could sell anything he wanted to, just by walking on the street and talking loudly about it." She had a faint smile on her face.

"Too bad he wasn't selling anything this time," I said. Which might have been what gave my mother her next idea.

A week later, she woke Lemuel and me early. We'd had no food at all the day before, only tea from plants she pulled from the garden. But it wasn't the season for harvest, and everything was expensive. When Lemuel complained last night at bed that he was too hungry to listen to a story about Father, she promised him that tomorrow, there would be food.

"Get dressed, Laman," she told me, and focused herself on dressing Lemuel.

I put on what I had worn the day before. I was afraid that if I allowed her to, Mother would wash all my clothes to rags when she went to the stones by the river. My other shirt had been ruined in just that way. I didn't care if it smelled so much as I cared that it was threadworn. No one could tell who was the one who stank when you walked in the street with hundreds of others.

"Not that!" said Mother when she turned around and saw me. She was smoothing the tunic over Lemuel's back, then running her fingers through his hair to straighten it. It had always looked disheveled, even before she sold our comb to buy food.

There was little left to sell now, except the house itself. And if she sold the house, how would Father find us again, if he came back? It wasn't that I believed that myself, but I knew that Mother and Lemuel did.

5

"What, then?"

"Your Sabbath clothes," she said, and pointed to the open box where she had taken out Lemuel's clothes. They were ridiculously small on him, because he had continued to grow in height since Father left, though he was much thinner.

Mother had seemed to grow hunched rather than thiner, and more pinched around the face. And her hair had gone grayer.

"I won't fit into those anymore," I said.

"Put them on," Mother said in that tone of voice that I had not heard much of lately. She was so rarely angry now. It heartened me. I thought that I knew what her plan was.

She would find Father in the street like we had before, only because we were looking for him this time, and she would shame him into coming home. She would shout at him and even beat at his face. I wanted to be there for that. I wanted to shout at him, too.

But once we were dressed, she licked her fingers and smoothed out my eyebrows. She reminded me to stand up straight. She told me to practice speaking properly, my words enunciated fully, the way that Father had always insisted.

And when we found him at last in the street, it was nearly dark. We had walked through the streets for hours, through the worst of the heat of the day. We'd had no water, for Mother would not let us stop our search to go find a stream to drink from. And of course, we'd still had no food.

He wasn't standing on a boulder now. There was no one surrounding him. He was lying on his back, a bottle of wine in his hand. I thought he was asleep when we first came upon him. I wouldn't have recognized him as my father if I hadn't been looking for him.

His beard was longer, and it was full of dirt, and I could see creatures living in it that made me want to pull away. His clothes were heavy and wet with urine. He reeked of wine and other smells that I did not want to think too carefully about.

"Lehi," said Mother, crouching down to touch him with a hand. "Oh, Lehi, how have you allowed yourself to come to this?"

That was all she was going to say to him? Not how could he allow her to starve and his sons to grow up without him? But how could he do this to himself?

"Come home with us. I can clean you up, at least," said Mother.

But Father batted her away. "Leave me be, Woman!" he said.

I saw later that there was a bruise on her face from where he touched her. He hurt her without even thinking about it. As if she were an insect.

"Laman!" said Mother. "Speak to your father. Beg him to come home."

I stood in front of him and stared down at him. He wasn't dancing now. He was muttering something to himself.

"God, I hear you." He shook his head. "No, please. Please, don't ask that of me. Anything but that. You can't know what it would mean to my family. My sons."

In his ravings, did he care about us, then? Maybe when you were crazy, you dreamed you were sane and cared about things like your wife.

"Laman, say something!" said Mother.

If she insisted, I would not disobey her. She was my mother, and she, at least, deserved my respect. "I hate you!" I said. And then I spat on him.

His hand went to his chest where my spittle had landed and dribbled down his filthy coat. He looked at me and I knew that he recognized me. But he did not say my name.

"Lemuel!" Mother cried out, turning to my younger brother since I had failed her. "Tell him to come home! Beg him! Tell your father you want to hear his stories again!"

Lemuel moved around me, obedient to our mother's urgent whispers. But what he said to Father was only this, "Please, do you have food? I'm hungry. Please."

Father patted at his clothes as if searching for a bag. But there was none. Finally, he looked at the dirt around him on the street and found a coin. He offered it to Lemuel, and Lemuel went off, delighted to find some bread. It was the right time of day to buy old bread, for it would be cheap and that one coin would buy plenty.

"We would welcome you home," said Mother. "All of us."

Father looked at me, and turned away. "I can't do it, Sariah. I'm not worthy of any of you."

He wasn't, and I suppose I knew that in that moment he wasn't as mad as I wished he was.

He came home four years after that. I had seen him in the street now and again, but always walked away from him. Sometimes he was laughing and drunk. More often, he was morose and as thin as we were. I felt some satisfaction in that.

When he came back, Mother found him on the doorstep in the morning. She had by then figured out how to make a living on her own. She'd taken in laundry from others, and mending, and did anything that would earn her a coin. Somehow, she'd managed to keep us in food and clothes, at least enough that we survived. And we kept the house.

A year after Father came back, we were wealthier than we ever had been before. Father paid off any debts Mother had incurred while he was gone. And then he bought us a new house, with so many rooms I didn't number them.

He convinced Mother that he was a changed man, and she welcomed him into her bed once more. Lemuel and I were almost grown, but I did not leave despite my feelings for my father. I felt that Lehi deserved to see the truth on my face every time I looked at him. And I deserved to have the advantage of some of his wealth when he realized he had a family again. It was my birthright.

He and Mother had two more sons, Sam and Nephi. I watched as they had everything I had never had. And they faced no deprivation ever. Father made sure of that. He doted on them. The perfect, loving father. That was the only man they knew.

He gave them all the time and attention in the world. He showered them with love, carried them on his shoulders when they were small, took them with him to the temple when they were older, read to them, and told them of his dreams.

Nephi and Sam went to sleep each night on those dreams, never realizing that what they heard were the excuses my father made to himself for being away from us for all that time. He told them of his dreams, of his spiritual journeys, of his conversations with God.

Fine. Let them have him. They had no idea, the fools. They did not know what was deep in his heart, the flaws and the weaknesses. I did.

We never spoke about those six years again, and they all pretended it had never been. Even Lemuel seemed to forget, though he had not been that young. I was the one who remembered the truth about my father, about God, and about prayers.

2

When Father returned, Lemuel and I mostly did what we wanted, and Father let us. We were bigger than he was by then. He used to be tall and strong, but six years on the street drunk hadn't done much for his physique. He shrank inside himself, all his muscles wasting away. He hunched over like an old man, and his hair went white.

When they were still little, Nephi and Sam liked to sit around on the floor in front of him, listening to him tell stories about the old prophets, about the glory days of Israel. He talked about Moses as if he had been there.

"Please, Lord, don't make me talk to people. I s-ss-ss-tu-tt-tt—ter and people laugh at me," said Father.

Nephi and Sam laughed at that and echoed his stuttering.

"You must tell the people the truth. You must make my people free," said Father, using his deep, echoing voice to be the Lord God of Israel.

That voice always made Nephi and Sam go very quiet.

"C—cc—cccan't you find someone else? I'm t—t—tt—oo weak. I just w—w—want to keep living my own life w—w—where I am," said Father as Moses.

The deep voice of God responded, "I am the one who saved your life. I kept you from being killed by the pharaoh. Don't you think that you owe me something in return for that? You lived a life of luxury and privilege all those years so that you could be educated enough to speak to the pharaoh. Now is the time for you to repay that debt."

Sometimes Father would find a scroll or two around the house that was part of the scriptures and he would read what he had of our history. He taught Nephi and Sam how to read and write properly, unlike me and Lemuel, who had been ignored and abandoned when we were at the age of learning skills that might have changed our future life paths. As grown adults, we were not going to ask Father to help us learn when we were grown men. We weren't going to make mistakes and sound like children.

And besides, what use were these scripts? It wasn't as if not knowing to read and write and not learning long sections of the old histories had kept us from being able to earn a living.

Yes, we lived with Father and Mother still, though we were grown men. We had not yet married, but we had our own businesses. We sold goods on the streets. Lemuel was an expert at shoes and other leather goods. He had spent some time apprenticing to a leather worker while Father was gone. I had spent my time with a man who taught me construction. I knew how to make bricks from mud and sand and I knew how to build a house so that it wouldn't fall down.

Mother would not speak of the six years when Father was missing. She would hush us if Lemuel or I brought it up. She would deny that it had ever happened. She stuck to the story that Father was gone for business and that he had returned as soon as he could. I could not even tell if she had made herself believe this or not. She protected him and she was as coddling of our two younger brothers as he was. What they did was all important. What we did was simply work for coins.

And did Father ever ask us about what we did? Did he ever apologize for the years he had been gone and we had had to make do for ourselves? No, he did not. Did he ever teach us the scriptures as it would have been fitting for men our age to learn them?

He danced around like Pharaoh in the Red Sea as it closed in on him, a spectacle for his favored children, who did not remember the part of his life that he should apologize for.

"Help me, Moses!" he screamed as he put his hands above his head and then slowly sank into the ground, as if the water could act like that. "I admit I was wrong. Speak to your God! Ask Him to forgive me! Moses, we were brothers once. You owe me one more chance. You—" And then, finally, he would die and be still.

Father would lie like that for a long while, until Nephi and Sam would stand up and poke at him, wondering if they could wake him up.

"Is he really hurt?" Sam would ask.

"He's still breathing," Nephi would say. "I can see his chest rising and falling."

"Why doesn't he get up?"

"He wants us to think about dying without God." Or some such.

Nephi was always the one who was trying so hard to win Father's approval. He strained so hard I sometimes thought he would burst open.

I felt sorry for him mostly, because I knew that one day Father would disappoint him the same way that he had disappointed Lemuel and me. One day, Father would be gone and Nephi would be completely unable to figure out what to do with his life without Father's approval shining down on him.

When Father went back to the streets and to his drinking, maybe then he'd come to me and ask for my advice. He'd see that Lemuel and I were the strong ones, not the rebellious and unfilial ones. Then we could talk about Father and his hypocrisy and laugh together about that.

But until then, I waited. And watched.

Sometimes Father took Nephi and Sam to the record-keeper, Laban, so that he could read to them out of the official scriptures. Sam and Nephi got so excited about that. It made me sick to see how solemn they looked. Father made them fast before they went, which should have made me happy, I guess. It was certainly the only time they suffered at all. But it wasn't real suffering. They always knew when they would get food again, and plenty of it. It was stupid to make two young boys go without food for no reason other than because it made Father feel proud of them.

They would make a procession to Laban's house, wearing their best white clothes, their heads covered and their voices shaking with want. Then they'd spend all day there, from sunup to sundown. Laban charged Father a healthy price for the privilege, though I was pretty sure he wasn't supposed to do that. The records were there for anyone in our family to see them, so long as they proved they could read.

But Laban was a man like any other. He had his own family and his own property to think about. He needed to earn money to keep them going, so why not take money from Father, who was so eager to give it away for the sake of piousness these days?

I tried to pull Nephi aside once and talk to him about the whole charade.

"Can't you see what he's doing? Father is just trying to make himself look good to you and Sam. He wants to make sure that when he is dead, you will write about how righteous a man he was."

"But he is righteous," said Nephi.

"You think he is, but you wait and see. He will show himself truly in time. You'll see how selfish he is."

Nephi looked at me with pity. I hated that he thought of me as the one who needed correction. "Laman, he has changed. He's heard God speak to him."

"Yes, and God told him to come home and have more sons. God told him to buy a new house and eat well. God told him to enjoy a good life. Convenient that what God wants and what our father wants are the same thing," I said.

"Didn't you change while Father was gone?" asked Nephi.

"Of course I changed. I was forced to change. I had to go out into the world and make my own living. I had to care for Mother because Father did nothing. I learned to depend on myself and to make sure I wasn't cheated or lied to by others." Like Father, I thought but did not say.

"Then it was good for you. Can't you see that? God wanted you to go through what you went through. He needed you to be strong. He has plans for your future, and all of this is leading to a grand design. When you see the end of it, you will understand why it had to be this way. You will rejoice with Father. He, too, was part of the story that will be told of your lives," said Nephi. His fists were tight and I could see his neck muscles straining. He wanted so much to believe what he said was true.

I did not find any comfort in it. What kind of God would want a father to leave his sons in a drunken stupor and to be gone for six years—useless? How had that been good for us? He could have stayed and taught us the same lessons that he was teaching Nephi and Sam. If God had wanted us to be righteous, He could have managed it without so much pain and suffering.

"I can't wait to see how God teaches you to be strong, then, little brother," I said, and walked away. We could not talk. Nephi simply could not understand what my life had been like, and I could not stand the way that he seemed to think he understood everything just because he knew how to read the ancient words of the prophets. How did that give him the right to tell me who God was and what my life was meant to be?

3

I got drunk that night. I didn't get drunk often, because I remembered Father being drunk and I didn't want to become him. But Father became more open and more boisterous when he was drunk. I became quieter and more sullen. I didn't go outside and start proclaiming things to the world when I was drunk. I drank purposefully and intently, to keep myself from thinking and feeling whatever thoughts and feelings were too much for me in the moment.

Lemuel came in after a few hours. I don't know how he knew what I was doing, but he did. He had a sense of how I felt and he came to cheer me up. Then as I talked to him about Nephi and Sam and about our father, he started to get melancholy and then he drank with me.

I had brought plenty to get two men drunk up to my room. It wasn't stolen or begged from anyone, unlike Father. And I wasn't going to hurt anyone. I hadn't married. I didn't have sons I was leaving neglected.

Father would hint every now and then that he thought it was time for me and Lemuel to start looking for brides. He offered to go and scout them out for us, bring them by for our approval.

As if we would let our father choose anything that mattered in our lives.

Lemuel and I simply went silent on the topic, refusing to say yes or no to anything he asked us. We had no intention of marrying. A wife would get pregnant soon enough, and then we would be weighed down by more burdens. Father had showed us how tempting it was to escape the chains of family. And how damaging.

But it didn't really matter to him. Because Father had Nephi and Sam to bring him grandsons and to carry on the family name. They would remember him as he wanted to be remembered. They would bring honor to him. They would be righteous and quote scriptures at his funeral. Lemuel and I would simply drift away as if we had never been.

Lemuel and I toasted each other and drank. We complained about Father and drank. We wrestled and wrecked furniture and drank. We pretended to be the perfect young sons that Father had now and we drank.

Somehow, in the midst of our drinking and play-acting, we knocked over a lamp. Then we were laughing so hard at how stupid we had been that we didn't do anything to stop the fire growing. It leaped from the rug on the floor to the curtains, and from there, to the chest and the bed.

When the bed caught fire, we realized we had to do something, so we started to throw off all the covers and try to smother them by turning them over. But it didn't work. Instead of stopping the fire on the bed, we drew the fire to ourselves and our clothes.

I saw Lemuel's trousers catch first, and I shouted at him. "Get out!"

He took a moment too long to glance down at himself, and then he was engulfed in flames.

I threw myself at Lemuel and tried to roll with him down the corridor away from the fire. More rooms were going up and I could hear servants shouting out in terror.

"Fire! Get out! Fire!" I shouted to all of them.

I tore off Lemuel's clothes with my bare hands, heedless of the blisters that immediately rose and then burst, dripping pus and blood down my arms. I carried him outside, and laid him down by the fountains in the courtyard, where it was cool and I thought unlikely for him to catch fire once more.

"Lem?" I shook him a bit, but he didn't answer.

Was he still alive? I tried to put a hand to his neck to feel for his blood rushing through, but my hands were too ruined to feel anything. I put my ear to his mouth and was sure I felt air coming in and out. He was alive, but badly hurt.

I wanted to go for a physician for him, but I could still hear cries coming from the west wing of the house. I had not intended for anyone else to be hurt and I was determined that I would not be like Father, heedless of those left behind. So I left Lemuel for the moment and went back into the fire.

I found one of the servant women with a babe in her arms, too terrified to get through the flames. I carried both of them, somehow finding strength I did not know I had. Then I went back and realized that the calls I heard were not from any servant but from Lemuel's dog, which he kept in his room, an old thing that Father had bought for him in those few good years before he left us. The creature should have put been down years ago, for she was blind and had only one good leg.

I couldn't leave her to burn to death, though. So I carried her out, though she bit me in her terror, and died while she lay at Lemuel's side as I watched that wing of the house burn down.

At least she was with him in the end, and he with her. I don't know if he remembered much else that night, but he remembered her licking his face until he woke up enough to see her, and then wrapped his arms around her neck and held her until she died.

I slumped to the floor and might have died there but for Father calling a physician. It is the one thing he did for me that showed that he cared at least about how it would look if he allowed his eldest son to die. When I woke, I was bandaged from head to foot and in some part of the house that I did not recognize at all. It was the east wing where Father lived with Mother, Nephi, and Sam, and their servants.

He had had it built shortly after we all moved in here, when he realized that it was not comfortable to have the two families together, pretending to be all harmony. He chastised Lemuel and me for our bad language dozens of times a day, always saying that it was inappropriate "in front of the young boys." He wanted everything different for them than it was for us. They ate only fresh fruits and vegetables, never any wine. They wore clothes he chose and woke and slept at the hours he designated.

I hated this wing of the house. It was unnaturally quiet. It stifled. I wanted to call out for someone to come talk to me, but I didn't. I kept quiet instead, and stared around the room.

Eventually, a servant came to bring a plate of broth and bread. When I asked for real food, she shook her head and said she couldn't bring me anything else.

"Where is Lemuel?" I asked her.

She shook her head again.

"My brother. He was in the fire with me. He must be somewhere near here." I was panicked that he had been hurt. Had he gone back into the fire? Was he dead? I had to know. He was the only person I considered my real family.

But the servant said she didn't know of my brother, that she had been hired to care for me only.

"Will you ask after him? Just tell me where he is and how he is doing. I need to know," I begged her. I couldn't live with myself if it meant living without Lemuel.

But the next time the servant came back, she said she had heard nothing of Lemuel. She insisted that I must rest and be quiet and think of nothing else.

As soon as she left, I tried to get out of the bed to go search for Lemuel. I couldn't get very far because of the stiff, heavy bandages on my legs, so I tore them off. That was when I got my first glimpse of what the fire had done to me. The skin was ruined. I could see where the scars would later form, making me hideous. I threw up, fell down, and knocked myself out.

I woke up again sometime later, back in bed, the bandages carefully reapplied, and the same servant scolding me for trying to get out of bed.

I asked her again about Lemuel. I asked her if Father would come to see me, or Nephi or Sam, or my mother. Anyone who could tell me about Lemuel. But she kept shaking her head and saying that I must rest and have quiet, and drink my broth.

I waited a few more days and then got out of bed again. This time, I left my bandages where they were. I walked slowly up and down the whole eastern wing of the house, poking my head into every door. But Lemuel was not there.

So I went outside. I got a sense of how horrible I looked in every face that walked down the street near me. I suppose I did not smell very good, either. I had not had a proper bath in weeks and the smell of my wounds, even well-cared for as they were, was not pleasant.

Just as well that I hadn't bothered to get married. If I had a wife, she would run screaming from me, and my children would think their father had become a monster.

Father would never marry me off now. It seemed a fitting revenge upon him, for thinking that such a thing was necessary for me to be happy in the future. I would never be happy now, and I could blame him forever for it.

I tried to call out Lemuel's name as I went down the street, but my voice was no more than a whisper and my lips could not move distinctly.

Several people bumped into me, twisting me this way and that, and I felt lost for a few moments, though I knew these streets very well, having lived here all my life.

I had to take a moment to lean over and rest, then made my way back home.

Was Lemuel dead? Was that he was no where to be found? And were they all too afraid of my reaction if they told me the truth?

I sagged back into my bed, sure that I had killed my own brother. I dreamt about Lemuel returning as a spirit to take me to task. I felt that he haunted my convalescent room. I began to spend hour after hour in silence, speaking as little as the servant who was there to care for me.

My mother did not come to visit me, nor my father. I suppose they were punishing me for my foolishness in causing the fire. They had every right to do this, and I would not have cared except that I was desperate to know what they knew about Lemuel. No one would tell me. I ached for the knowledge, even of his death, but I was left ignorant.

Weeks passed, and at last, Nephi and Sam came to visit me. They came without Father and when I asked where he was, Nephi said, "He's visiting Lemuel."

In my despair, I thought that must mean that Father was visiting the graveyard where Lemuel was buried. Had he been given a good stone to mark his place? Would I be allowed to visit it? I had loved my brother so much that I could not imagine being parted from him. I should have died with him. I wished I had died.

To entertain me, Nephi and Sam started to act out one of the scenes from the scriptures, the one with Moses and the soldier he killed.

"Get out!" I shouted at them. My throat had healed enough now that I realized I could shout, and my voice sounded thunderous.

Nephi and Sam scuttled away, and I spent weeks longer alone, feeling sorry for myself, though I knew I deserved it.

When after some time Lemuel appeared in my doorway, I was sure that he had come as a spirit to bring me to the after-life with him. His face was untouched by scars, and I didn't see anything on his arms because he was wearing long sleeves. I remembered that Father had told us that if we died and had been righteous enough to return to God, our bodies would be perfected, that all our wounds would be healed. I thought that was what had happened to Lemuel.

"I am ready," I said, and held out my hands. I was tired of being in this bed, tired of broth and bread, tired of a servant who was too afraid to speak to me, tired of myself and my own thoughts.

"Good. You've been here too long," said Lemuel. He reached out an arm and pulled me to my feet and I thought how strange it was that he felt so real, his body so sturdy. Surely spirits were not like that—unless you were a spirit, as well.

I looked back, expecting to see my ruined body still on the bed, but it was gone.

"You should see your face!" said Lemuel. "You look like you've seen a ghost."

"Then you're not—" I said.

"I'm alive." He pulled up his sleeves and showed me his scars. They were much less extensive than mine.

"Then where were you?" I asked. "Why were you not here, in the house? I looked for you."

"Father sent me to a physician." He showed his foot to me and I could see now that he was missing several toes. "He was worried I would never walk again. But here I am, proving him wrong." His eyes shone at me, as if inviting me to join in his laughter.

I couldn't. I turned away from him, consumed by guilt that he had suffered so, that I had not protected him as the eldest brother should do for the younger.

Lemuel kept telling me over and over again that he didn't mind missing several toes, that everything was fine. He tried to dance for me and show me that he was as good as ever, but he fell over and then laughed and said that if he wasn't as good as ever, it didn't matter. It wasn't as if he needed to be able to walk or run to do anything that he cared about.

It took several more weeks for me to get out of bed and talk to Lemuel again. But I've never forgiven myself for that. Of all the terrible things that I've done in my life, I am most sorry for that one. I love Lemuel more than any-one else in the world. He knows me better than anyone else. And did that save him from being hurt by me?

No. I am no better than Father, in the end. I complain about him all the time, but we share the same weaknesses. Watching Father with Nephi and Sam now, I see what he is doing with them. They are his second chance to do things right. They are his redemption. I wish that I had some hope of redemption, but I don't see how.

4

I offered more than once to help Father rebuild the west wing, since it was my fault it was ruined. I had money that I had been saving up to move out of the house and the skills and connections to do it quickly and cheaply.

Father put me off a few times, told me once rather curtly that he wasn't interested, and then one day called the whole family together. I thought that he was going to say that I must move out on my own, that he could not trust me to be in the same house with his beloved sons. I was prepared to go, prepared to feel no pain at the announcement, but instead, he said that he'd had a dream.

"It was a dream from God."

As soon as he said that, I started watching him for the signs that he was back to his old drunken ways. I thought I would see him sway from side to side, that his words would be slurred. But they weren't. He seemed as normal as he had been since he returned to us.

Nephi and Sam were looking up at him as if he were some kind of prophet, young and so vulnerable.

"How can you be so sure it was from God?" I asked suspiciously.

But no one paid any attention to my questions, not even Lemuel.

"God Himself was in the dream," said Father. "He came to me and stood before me, like a man stands before another man. He was wearing a white gown and his feet were bare, as my feet were. I knelt down before Him, but He touched me and told me to stand and listen. And then He spake and told me that Jerusalem was to be destroyed. In not more than two years hence, all who remained here would be captured and turned to slaves by a greater nation. And God said that He would allow this to happen in order to teach His children more humility and obedience. He said that His prophets have been ignored for too long and that the wickedness of this city is too great."

"Then what do we do?" asked Nephi. "Do we go around and tell people to repent? Will that stop us from being slaves?"

"I don't want to be a slave," said Sam.

We all saw slaves in the marketplace on a regular basis, those who had been sold to pay for debts, or who had been taken from other kingdoms as chattel.

"I have already cried repentance to this people. For years, I have tried to get them to listen to me, but it has had no effect. They do not want to hear God. They do not want the fruits of righteousness. They have already made their choice."

I thought about Father's drunken calls to people to repent and wondered if that was what he thought was sufficient warning to Jerusalem that God was about to destroy the city and send the survivors to be slaves? Or had he done more than that?

I wasn't so sure that I believed this dream of his, and I was his own son. Why should anyone else listen to an old man who has been known as a raving drunk for most of his life?

"We must pack up our things and be ready to flee to the wilderness. As Moses and his people fled Pharaoh, so we will flee—until God tells us how to get to our own Promised Land flowing with milk and honey."

"I thought this was the Promised Land," I said. I thought it was funny, and laughed a bit.

No one else joined in.

"God decides what land is promised. And this land is now cursed for the sake of the wicked. We must go where God sends us now. He will be our protector and our guide."

"And you'll be His translator?" I said. Mother was listening to this as intently as anyone else. Did she want to go into the desert at her age? And for what? So that Father could pretend to have more visions? Was he going to give up his wine, at least? Or would we be bringing plenty of that along, too?

"We're supposed to trust you that you will understand everything God says to you? What happens when we run out of food? When we can't find water?"

"God will lead us. We will find animals to hunt and eat," said Father. "You must trust in God."

I had less trouble trusting in God than I did in trusting in my father.

"I will follow you, Father," said Nephi. He was about fourteen years old. He was nearly as tall as Lemuel was now, and I thought about how easy his life had been. He could trust in Father because he had never seen Father at his worst.

But what was I supposed to do? I had hurt Lemuel. He was missing toes. How would he fare in the wilderness? And what about Mother? What would happen to her when we ran out of food? She'd make sure that Nephi and Sam had food and pretend she wasn't hungry. She'd do it until she died. I knew she would.

Nephi and Sam thought they were so strong and righteous. But when things went badly, they'd ask me to take charge. Because I was the eldest. I was the one they would think should know the answers. And I knew nothing about the wilderness.

"If you want to see my dream and know if it is from God, I have been told to counsel all of you to ask God for the dream yourselves. He will send it to you this very night, if you are ready to see it."

I saw Nephi and Sam nodding, and we all went to bed that night quietly, in fasting because Father said that would help us receive the vision.

I don't know about the others. Nephi and Sam claimed to have seen everything that Father had seen. Lemuel nodded a few times and didn't say much.

Later, when we were alone, he admitted to me that he had seen a few snatches of what seemed a vision, though he wasn't absolutely sure if it had been colored by what Father had told him. What if he only dreamed what he dreamed because he was hungry and because it was the last thing he was thinking about before he went to bed?

As for me, I saw nothing at all that night nor any night after. I knew Father would have told me it was because I wasn't righteous or humble enough to receive God's word. But I believed it was because I wasn't as easily led as the rest of them. And wasn't that a good thing? That I could see the difference between what was real and what was imagined?

But when it came down to it, I went with them. I couldn't bear to think of Mother and Nephi and Sam in the wilderness alone with Father. They'd never survive and I would feel guilty all the rest of my life. I had chosen never to marry, but they were still my family, no matter how stupid I thought they were being. I suspected I might have been able to get Lemuel to stay with me, if I had tried hard enough. But as much as I owed him, I couldn't think only of us.

We took a full day to pack. Then the next morning, we were off. I made sure to eat a good meal when we left. Father told the servants that we were leaving, and told them what of our things they could have, for being good servants. They wept and told him that they would stay in the house for him, and keep it going until he came back. He told them that he wasn't coming back, but why should they believe him?

How long did I think our Father could actually last in the wilderness? I estimated we'd be out of the house for a night and maybe half of a day. Then we'd come home and Father would say that we'd passed his little test, and he'd give us some reward. Or he would if Lemuel and I could keep our mouths shut. Not that our reward would be anything like what he would give Nephi and Sam, but at least it would be something. Maybe it would be worth it.

"This is ridiculous," I said, as we went out the city gates.

"Think of it as an adventure," said Lemuel. "It will make great stories to tell the ladies."

Since his toes had been cut off, Lemuel had shown more interest in women. Instead of being repulsed by his wound, they were all fascinated by his foot and Lemuel always had new stories to tell them about how it had happened. Sometimes it was a lion he had tried to tame. Other times it was an angry camel. Or a lightning bolt that had struck him. Or a cart that had run over him as he was trying to save a frightened child.

"There won't be stories to tell if we all die," I said.

"Then you make sure we don't die," said Lemuel.

"While Father has more dreams and visions?" I asked.

Lemuel shrugged. "Father is who he is. He's not going to change."

"Then why do we always have to be the ones to change around him?"

"Because we are fated to be his sons," said Lemuel. He had started saying things like this more often.

I suspected that he had tried to learn how to read Father's scripture scrolls. I noticed that Father had taken none of them with us. We didn't have room for them. At least he was being practical in one way.

The strange thing was that while I expected Father to soon be complaining about how much his legs hurt, how hot it was, and how he needed to rest, he actually seemed to grow stronger with every step we took away from home. Stronger and taller and more sure of himself.

I couldn't figure out how he even knew where we were going. The desert all looked the same to me, an endless stretch of sand. When I could turn back and see Jerusalem in the distance, that kept me sane. But as soon as the city was gone, I was utterly lost. What did Father think he was doing?

That night, he directed us on how to set up the tents. There was one for Mother and Father and Nephi and Sam. A separate one for me and Lemuel. In the middle of the desert, where windstorms came and covered whole cities of people, and what did we have to protect us? A bit of cloth and Father's promise that God would protect us, because God had plans for our future.

"Where are we going?" I asked Father that night. If Lemuel and I had some idea of where we were headed, we could scope it out.

"The Lord will reveal it to me," said Father.

"So, you have no idea even which direction we're supposed to head in?" I was trying not to be angry about this, but I guess I wasn't succeeding.

"You need to learn to be obedient. God told me to leave Jerusalem, and I left. God told me to live in a tent, and I will live in a tent until He tells me what to do next," said Father.

"We could go back home now," I said. "God could speak to you there. You did what He asked you to do, didn't you?"

"Laman, there is no going home. We will never see Jerusalem again. You must accept that," said Father.

"Because Jerusalem is going to be destroyed, right? Well, I bet if we went back right now, it would still be standing. Do you want me to go right now and prove it to you? I could go home and find our house still standing and bring back Mother's bed for her. That would make her more comfortable out here in the sand."

"We need nothing but God," said Father.

He wasn't the one who had to watch Mother trying to find a soft spot to lie down her head. I could not understand why she had taken Father back when he came home all those years ago. Well, I did understand, but it made me grit my teeth. She loved him and as a woman, she was not considered whole without her husband and the father of her children at her side.

"Mother, don't you want to go home?" I asked her as I helped her into her bed. She was shaking so badly she could hardly lie in it. She hadn't done this much walking in her whole life.

"I will follow my husband where he leads me," she said, closing her eyes.

"He is a fool. At least say that out loud. That he is a dreamer and half-mad with wanting to be a prophet of

God." It was the only thing that Father could hope for now. He wasn't going to be a leader of any of the tribes. He had offended everyone far too much for that.

"He is a dreamer, but I believe his dreams are true," said Mother.

Why wouldn't she speak the truth? "Dreams are dreams. They mean nothing," I said. "Mother, I know that he is your husband, but we may all die out here. Are you not worried about that?"

"Then I will die in his arms. And in the Lord's eyes," said Mother. "Laman, forgive him the past. See him as the man he has become. Then you will be at peace, too."

And would I be content to die so long as I was with him? I didn't think so.

"I will keep you safe, Mother," I promised her. I don't think she heard me, because she was already asleep. Her body was still twitching and trembling with exhaustion, though. I put my hands on her legs and rubbed at them until they lay still once more.

And it was only then that Father came into the tent. He said he had been praying, and thanked me for my care to my mother. Then he told me to go into my own tent and pray once more to see the dream he had seen. "For it will give you peace and purpose, my son. It will show you God's love and His plan for your life."

I prayed as I had prayed before. But God was as silent as ever.

In the morning, we woke and rose to strike down the tents.

Mother bent over and folded the fabric of the tent as Father took up the stakes. I thought how wrong she looked here. Her hair was gray, her body worn out, her eyes red from fighting the sand in them, her hands spotted with age.

But Father turned to her as she stumbled, caught her, and told her that she would one day be known as the Mother of prophets, a woman of God, a voice in the wilderness. She would be like Eve and like Esther and Ruth, a woman written of in scriptures.

"How can she be written of when we have no skins to write on? We brought nothing with us to write scriptures? You never thought of that," I pointed out.

Father's face burned with anger, and told me that I would have no dinner that night, so that I could fast and learn humility before a prophet of God.

He could not stop me from eating whatever I wished. I ate openly of a bird I had trapped by myself, for I had far more experience in living off the land than he did. I was the one who had kept Lemuel and Mother alive while he was gone.

When I was finished, I belched loudly and went to my tent, listening only dimly to the sound of Father's earnest stories about the scriptures to the others. It was the same as before. It always would be.

5

After dinner that night, which burned badly over the ambitious fire that Nephi and Sam had made, I predicted "We'll go home tomorrow."

"I hope so," said Lemuel. "I'm thirsty and it's going to be hot at midday. My feet are blistered and all I want to do is get a massage." He took off his sandals and showed me his burned and blistered feet.

"Why is he doing this, do you think?" I asked.

"Father?" Lemuel shrugged. "I think he's starting to worry that Nephi and Sam are going to turn into us."

"Yeah, and that would be a horrible fate, wouldn't it?" I said. Sam had started to refuse to show up at scripture time in the last few months, and I'd heard him backtalk Father more than once. He didn't believe that Father knew the scriptures as well as he claimed. He said he wanted to study with someone else, and Father said that the other teachers were all heretics, and didn't believe in the true God.

I wondered how much Father's objections had to do with money. It was a lot cheaper for him to teach the scriptures himself than it was to pay for lessons with one of the official teachers.

"Even Nephi is starting to make his own account of all of this. Did you know that? He says that he doesn't trust Father to get it all right. He thinks that Father forgets important parts and doesn't put in anything that Nephi himself does," said Lemuel.

I laughed at that. Nephi was complaining that Father didn't give him enough credit? I guess if we survived all of this desert living, scribes of the future could argue about who was right for millennia to come.

"Too bad we don't know how to write anything," I said to Lemuel.

"Yeah, well, now we know the danger of teaching our children anything," said Lemuel. "It's just a way for them to rewrite our lives and prove us wrong."

"Luckily for us, that won't be a problem. Because who would marry either of us?" I asked Lemuel. Obviously, out in the wilderness, we'd never marry. But even if we went back to Jerusalem, who would want to marry sons of a man who was known to be insane?

"Maybe we could find some scorpions," said Lemuel, gesturing out at the sand. "Or possibly a she-lion."

"You take the she-lion. I'll take the scorpion," I said. "I think I prefer the quicker death."

"You know, there might be women out in the wilderness whose fathers also had a vision to leave Jerusalem," said Lemuel, grinning at me. He seemed to still be having a fine time.

"Any sane woman would tell her father she'd rather stay home in Jerusalem, whatever the risks of invasion," I said.

"Or she might be sweet and biddable," said Lemuel. "That's what I hope for."

I rolled my eyes at that. "And that one will marry Nephi or Sam," I said. "We'll get the older sisters with the warts on their noses and the bad breath."

There was a long silence.

"Do you really think that we'll never get married?" asked Lemuel in a humbler voice.

"I think it's pretty likely at this point. I wouldn't marry us, so how could I blame any women who feel the same way? We're getting past the ideal age, for one thing. And we're not nearly as handsome as Nephi and Sam," I said bluntly.

"Well, we could take both of them in a fight," said Lemuel, punching his fists into the air.

"A fair fight?" I asked, dubious.

"I didn't say anything about that," said Lemuel with a smirk. "However we win, it's who's standing at the end that matters, right?"

"I think Nephi might say differently." Not to mention our father.

"Who cares what he says?" said Lemuel.

"Well that's another problem. He's smarter than we are. He learns faster. He would do better in just about any business than either of us would." This was pretty depressing, thinking about. Any woman who even considered us would want Nephi first. Which meant we had to get him married off before us, so he wasn't competition. Sam, too.

Unless they were both out here in the desert and we weren't.

"No wonder he's everyone's favorite," Lemuel said glumly.

Why were we out here again in the middle of the desert? Father's dream, which I hadn't had and Lemuel wasn't very committed to. And because of Mother.

I loved Mother. I did. But I wasn't sure that I was willing to give up the rest of my life to protect her. Or that I could, if Father was determined to stay out here in the wilderness until everyone died.

I could go back home, take over the house, convince the servants to come back. There was enough of value there that I could survive for a little while just by selling things. And I could go back into my own business, if I wanted to. Or take over Father's. Or do both, if Lemuel was willing to come along with me.

What reason did I have to stay here and be abused? I hadn't had a vision. God, if He existed, didn't care about me. He wanted Nephi and Sam here, not me and Lemuel. Everyone would just be happier if we separated. Father would hardly miss us except for the daily lectures he gave about proper behavior and devotion to God.

I felt a little guilty about leaving Nephi and Sam out here with him. Sure, they thought they were doing the right thing by being obedient to Father. They were annoyingly self-righteous about it all. But what if they died and I wasn't here to help them? How would I feel about that in twenty years, if no one ever came home? I'd know what happened to them, and I'd know it was my fault.

Nephi and Sam were like children still. I had never felt particularly close to either of them. We didn't share views or interests. But they were my brothers. They were my blood. I loved them.

I might not like them, but I loved them and I didn't want to abandon them. But how could I get them to listen to reason? Maybe we could come back for them in a few days, when they were willing to listen to reason.

Lemuel and I left Father's camp together in the middle of the night, utterly silent. There was really no other choice.

6

Leaving was supposed to feel triumphant, but it only lasted for about a hundred feet. Then the sand started filling our shoes and got heavier and heavier with every step. We didn't dare look back, so we kept focused forward, kept trudging onward.

Even when the sun rose and it burned into us, it still seemed better than turning around and going back, admitting that we were wrong. I really hoped we were going in the right direction.

"We'll get married," said Lemuel. "We're going to be rich enough that lots of women won't even care what we look like."

"Or what we smell like," I said dourly, not nearly as optimistic as he was about our current desert location. Were we even sure where the city was relative to us? We were just guessing at this point. We had neither map nor compass.

"When we have children of our own, we'll have fun with them. We'll actually play with them instead of leaving them on their own." Lemuel was gritting his teeth as he trudged through the sand, sweat dripping down his face.

"No teaching scriptures or anything boring. We'll teach them how to steal from other merchants and how to run away. And we'll take them camel racing in the desert. And always make sure we have enough to eat and drink," he added.

If we survived this. If we ever saw Jerusalem again.

"People will come to us and ask us for advice," Lemuel said. "And we'll tell them how to make money. Lots and lots of money. We'll be governors. Respected men. People will come to us before praying to God because we get real results."

I was trying to think about when we'd start seeing the outline of the city ahead of us? It had only taken us half a day of walking to get to our campsite. Where was it? Why couldn't we see it now? I had a sinking feeling that God had intervened to make sure that we were walking in circles, but I couldn't see footprints in the sand.

I stopped for a moment and told Lemuel I needed to take a bearing.

"I think it's that way," said Lemuel, pointing ahead of us.

I squinted. I couldn't see anything.

"We just have to keep walking away from the camp. It's a straight line from there to Jerusalem," I said, and tried to find Father's tent behind us. But I couldn't see that, either.

"Are we lost?" asked Lemuel.

I shrugged. I didn't want to admit to it, but I was very much afraid that's what we were. Maybe we deserved to die. Maybe this was God's plan to get us away from Father and our two more blessed younger brothers, who were supposed to go to the Promised Land.

"You idiot!" Lemuel shouted.

I was tired and hot and ready to fight. I turned around and put my face close to Lemuel's. "I'm the idiot? You know, you could have stopped walking with me any time along the way if you had any better ideas." He was too busy thinking about how great our lives would be when we got back to Jerusalem to actually do anything to help us get there.

He didn't back away. He didn't even blink. "I thought you knew where you were going. You acted like you knew everything."

He wanted to believe that I knew everything because that was easier. "We can just sit down here and wait for Sam and Nephi to find us," I said. I was sure that they had found out we were missing hours ago. But that wasn't a guarantee that they cared. Or that Father did. Or God.

Lemuel turned for a moment to look into the distance.

"Look, we can just follow the path of the sun. It moved from east to west. And Jerusalem is due west of the camp in the desert. I think." It was close to due west, anyway. If I could figure out which way due west was.

Lemuel turned back and threw the first punch. "We're going to die. And it's all your fault, you idiot!" He threw me on the ground and we started pummeling each other. "Father said we'd end up in hell, burning to death, and now we are."

It was hard to imagine a hell that would be worse than this. I gave up fighting back and let Lemuel keep hitting at me. My head was jolting into the sand again and again.

Finally, Lemuel gave up, pushed me away from him, and rolled to the side. He was breathing hard and sweating even harder.

"You probably just killed yourself," I whispered to him. "All that energy you used up. All that sweat dripping off you is water you might not be able to replace. You're the idiot."

"Am not," said Lemuel.

"Are too," I said, and then started to laugh weakly. I know. We sounded like four year-olds. I wished we still were that young, back in Jerusalem, with nothing but the next meal to worry about. You can go without food for a long time. Not so much with water.

"So what do we do now?" asked Lemuel.

"I guess we could pray for a vision," I said, only half-joking.

"God doesn't speak to people like us," said Lemuel.

He was right about that. So, on to the next choice. "We could try to go back." And then what? Bow our heads whenever Father said anything stupid that was supposed to come from God? Let our younger brothers rule over us?

Lemuel didn't answer. He liked this idea as little as I did.

"Or we could keep trying to go back to Jerusalem. We'll probably make it there eventually."

Lemuel looked up at the sky. "It's mid-afternoon. We could find some shade and wait until night. Maybe we'll see something then."

I doubted we'd see anything then. But it would be easier to travel at night. "There's some trees up ahead," I said. I could at least see that much.

So we managed to make our way to the trees, which offered a bit of shade.

I was so thirsty I couldn't help but think of the fruit Father had packed to go with us. If only I had thought to take those with us, we could have kept going. I hadn't wanted to steal anything, though. I'd felt bad because it might mean life or death for the rest of them. I hadn't realized it might mean life or death for us, too.

"Now what?" asked Lemuel.

"Take a nap?" I said.

Lemuel thought about arguing for a moment—I could see it in his eyes. Then he gave it up, closed his eyes, and proceeded to do just that. He curled up, pulled his robe over his head to block out the sun, and started to snore.

I closed my eyes, but I couldn't sleep, so instead I tried to imagine what I would do when I got back to Jerusalem.

First, I would take a bath. In cool, fresh water. Then I would drink cold wine. I would eat freshly cooked meat, well-seasoned. After that, I could lie down and have a servant come fan me while I slept. Maybe I could go to the market and buy a stream. Or a house by a stream. We could sell Father's.

I couldn't hear Lemuel snoring anymore, which seemed like a good thing. Until I realized that I couldn't hear my own voice, either. The only thing I could hear was a roaring sound in my ears, and it felt like something was pushing at me and tearing at my clothes.

I opened my eyes and realized that we were in the midst of a sandstorm. The wind was whipping around us pretty badly. We'd heard of sandstorms in Jerusalem, but they rarely affected us other than delaying traders who were moving across the desert—or killing them so that what we bought was more expensive due to increased demand and decreased supply.

"Sandstorm!" I shouted, and poked Lemuel awake.

He started and looked like he might try to tackle me again. Then the wind blew him forward so that he fell onto his face, and he stopped trying to get at me and started trying to keep his footing.

"We have to keep the wind from blowing us away!" I shouted, but I don't think Lemuel heard me. I wrapped my arms around his arms, putting our faces together. I could see the fear stamped into his wide eyes. I had brought him to this. I was an idiot. This was all my fault.

I was the eldest and I was supposed to know the most important things, like how to tell if a sandstorm is coming.

"Mother!" Lemuel shouted. "And Father."

Yes, they would likely be in this sandstorm, too. Was the camp they had chosen any better a place to weather this storm than where we were? If we could get back to it, we might survive as a group more easily than if we were alone.

But every time I tried to take a step in any direction, I felt as if the wind was going to tear me into pieces. We dug our feet into the sand and felt our robes being whipped around us, cut into pieces like some great beast was toying with us.

The noise of the storm alone was enough to make me wish that I never saw the desert again. But it wasn't just the noise. My ears, nose, and mouth were filled with sand. Every time I tried to swallow, it felt like I was gagging. But I dared not let any fluid past my throat. I had to keep it down. It was my only hope of survival.

Heat from the pounding sun was no longer my top concern. I was just worried that we would be buried in sand, never to breathe again. My only focus was this breath, and the next one. I put the rags that were all that remained of my robes to my face to cover it, and tried to breathe through them, until the rags were gone. Then I used my hands.

Soon, I could see my hands dripping blood from the wild force of the wind, but I kept them up until it seemed that the blood mixed with the sand and created a kind of scab. I could not feel my fingers anymore. They seemed to belong to someone else. But I kept upright, too terrified that if I so much as dropped to one knee, the sand would pour over me and bury me.

Lemuel felt like a statue made of sand next to me. I did not know if he was still living. I could not see if he was moving or if he had been dried like one of the Egyptian mummies that we had paid to see in the days after Father returned home and we had money to spend on such luxuries.

It might have been only hours or it might have been days that we remained like this. I do not know. I was sure that we were going to die there. The sound of the wind around us made it impossible to speak, and I felt lonelier than I ever had in my life. There was nothing to do but hope—and pray.

I had never prayed to Father's God before. I had never seen any point to it. Mother had prayed when Father was gone. She had prayed every night and I had seen how little purpose there was in any of it. It didn't make him come back. It didn't bring food to us. It didn't give her the respect of those who looked down upon her—upon all of us. So what was the point?

But maybe when you're really desperate, you're ready to try anything.

"Please, let us live," I prayed silently, my lips moving with the words I couldn't hear. "Great God of all Israel, great God who delivered our ancestors from the slavery of Pharaoh, great God who saved us from the flood, and who watches over all the world, I beg you to let these two humble children live."

I heard no answer. What did I expect? That God would speak to me now, when He had decided to punish me for rejecting my father and his dream?

So I made a bargain. Mother always made a bargain with God, and it seemed to me that the sacrifices that were left for God in the temple were the same thing. If you wanted God to do something for you, you offered him something in return. This sacrifice for a good harvest. This offering for the promise that your son will live long and healthy on the earth. This dance for the hope of your daughter's prospects for a husband.

"If you let us live, I promise that we will follow Father all the way into the wilderness. We will go to the Promised Land with him. We will go with him no matter what he asks us to do. We will be obedient sons, the way he wants us to be. We will act like Nephi and Sam, and bow our heads meekly and say that we love him. All this I swear. Let us live, and we will be changed men, reborn." I prayed variations on this again and again through the hours of the sandstorm.

And though I cannot say that I heard an answer like a voice in my head, I felt something. I do not know what it was. Perhaps it was no more than my imagination. But I felt as if arms enfolded me. Huge, warm arms made of flesh and blood.

I had never thought of my father's God as a man like I was, like my father himself was. If you had asked me what he was like, I would have said that He was elemental, that He was made of light and air and water, but perhaps not earth. I would have said that He was beyond my comprehension. Or perhaps that He was made of spirit and light, like the stars themselves.

I felt pressed to a chest, though, and I was sure I could feel another heart beating next to mine. And it was not Lemuel's, because his heart had to have fluttering as anxiously as mine was, and this heart was safe and sure. This heart was deep and wide enough to fill an ocean, yet delicate enough to answer my own blood's question.

I love you, the heart told me. And the pressure of the arms. And the chin that I felt just above the top of my head.

I love you, I heard without a voice. *Though you run from me. Though you do not trust me. Though you do not know my language and do not read of my words to others. Though you have evil thoughts. Though you hate your brothers and your father, who are my prophets. Though you will do evil all your days. Though you may not repent or grow wiser or kinder or greater than you are.*

Still, I love you.

It was perhaps that sense of peace and belonging that kept me alive during the last part of the storm more than anything else. I lost all sense of up and down, of time, of place. I forgot why I was here or where I had come from. I knew only that I was with someone who was greater than the storm, and that I could wait for as long as the storm lasted.

7

All too soon, the arms let go of me and I felt as if I was stumbling about, blind. I couldn't stand upright and I fell into the cutting sand.

It was the middle of the night, pitch-black, and when I recovered myself enough to think of my name, and my father's name, and my history, I could see a light in the distance. It was not a star, but it looked to me like someone in Jerusalem had hung a thousand lamps just for me, so that I could see how to get there.

Except that I was not going back to Jerusalem. Because I had made a promise to God.

It seemed to me as if He was saying to me that the choice was mine, even so. Despite the fact that I had made the bargain, I could still choose to return home to the easy life—for as long as it lasted—or I could choose to continue on Father's sacred journey to some unknown Promised Land. I could choose to honor my bargain or not.

"Lemuel?" I croaked out.

I heard a voice nearby, and then the sound of a cry, followed by the thump of body hitting ground.

I put out my hands and called out again, making my way on hands and knees toward him. "Lemuel?" I said again.

"Laman," he said in answer, a sigh of relief.

"We're alive," I said.

"Did you feel something in the storm?" said Lemuel.

"Hands. Protection," was all I could get out.

"I don't want to go back to Father," said Lemuel.

I didn't, either. But I wasn't sure that I could not do it, either. Not after what had happened to me. Was it anything like one of Father's dreams? It couldn't be, surely. Father saw things in his dreams. He heard things. God spoke to him. I hadn't been worthy of any of those things.

"We have to go back," I said, my voice ragged, but certain.

I was prepared for Lemuel to fight me again, but he didn't. "I'm afraid," he said, and his voice was as small as a child's. "What will happen to us? What other dangers will we face?"

I didn't know. I was afraid, too. Or a part of me. Another part of me didn't fear anything, so long as I could remember the feeling of those arms around me, that heart beating in my ear, and that voice in my head that said, "I love you."

"Come, Lemuel," I said.

We walked away from the lanterns that indicated Jerusalem across the desert. Somehow, I felt sure of every step and never stopped to rest or to check our direction.

"Do you think Father prayed for us?" I asked Lemuel, at one point.

"That God would send a storm to stop us and send us back?" asked Lemuel.

"Something like that," I said. I wasn't sure if that would make me happier about what I was doing now or not. Did Father have the power to call down God like that? Wouldn't that make me want to be more like him, so that I could wield that power myself? Or so that I could avoid others using it against me?

"It didn't feel like it came from Father," said Lemuel. "He would have been angry with us."

Lemuel was right about that. There had been no anger in those arms. It made me feel better to think that. Perhaps Father's God was our God, as well. Perhaps it didn't take Father to speak to Him for us. Perhaps we could do it on our own, when we were in our need. And He would save us, if only we asked Him. Because He loved us, just as it had seemed He was saying to us without words.

It was early the next morning when we made it back to Father's camp. I did not ask if they had faced the same storm we had. But we found Father, Mother, Sam, and Nephi, all packed up and waiting for us to go. Sam was carrying our tent.

Lemuel went over and took it away from him. He was in a better mood than I was, for some reason. God saved us, and He loved us, but that didn't mean anything about how we had to feel about our younger brother.

"God told me in the night that he would send you back to us, and so we waited," said Father. "All day we waited and into the next night."

I didn't know what to say to that, so I said nothing. I couldn't find words for the experience we'd had in the sandstorm and I knew that Father would take it as proof that he was right. I trusted God, but not my father in that moment.

Father nodded at Mother and Nephi and Sam. Then we started walking.

I began to pray differently that day, as the sun rose and baked the heat into us. I should have prayed for relief, for God to give us what we needed. I didn't. I prayed to die.

"Let us die. Let us die soon. This minute," I prayed. There was nothing more I wanted than the respite death could bring to us. I was tired of walking, tired of the heat, tired of hearing Father encourage Mother to keep going.

And then I fell forward and thought that I would never get up again. It took a moment before I realized that I had landed in water. I sputtered and splashed and nearly drowned, so startled was I.

Then I scrambled out, the water feeling as delicious to me as any wine I had ever had. I dipped my head back in and drank until I could drink no more.

I will always give you what you need, even if you do not ask, I heard a voice speaking into my head again. But before I could reach for it or speak back, it was gone.

I could see Father helping Mother kneel down so that she could dip her hands in. I could see Sam and Nephi playing around, dunking each other in. But Lemuel was with me. He'd already had his fill, and he was just lying at the side of the river as it stretched out on its journey to the open sea.

I realized then I didn't need our house with its beautiful furniture and its walls and rugs and tapestries. I didn't need all the fine clothing we had left behind. I didn't need wine or well-seasoned meat or good bread, freshly baked. I didn't need all the things that I had been so angry about Father leaving behind.

I needed water.

I needed Lemuel. He was my only real family, my truest brother, my dearest friend.

I needed my body. My face, to see and to taste and to smell. My hands to reach. My legs to move. My mind, to enjoy. My lungs to breathe.

And all of these, God had given me, though I had not asked Him. He knew me and He loved me, just as He'd said in the storm.

8

That feeling of perfect well-being lasted until I began to vomit. I wanted to keep the water down, but I had taken in too much at once. After I lay, utterly exhausted, on the bank for an hour or more, Lemuel helped me to get to the water again, and this time, I only drank a couple handfuls at a time. I waited for long minutes, then drank a bit more.

Mother and Father were anxious to set up our tents again, but I couldn't help. Lemuel worked on our tent while I lay useless on the bank of the river. Nephi set up the tent for Mother and Father, but Sam sat next to me.

"Nephi says that we are going to be in the desert for a long time," said Sam. "He said that God told him it would be many years."

"Wonderful," I said, wishing that I could tell Nephi what I thought about him and his unfailing self-righteousness and certainty right now.

Then Sam surprised me. He whispered, "I don't like being in the desert. There's sand in everything. My hair, my clothes, my feet, even in my foot. The water even tastes like sand. Why would God ask us to live in the desert for years? We're not like the ancient Israelites. We don't need to all die here so that our children can be righteous. Do we?" He glanced back at Nephi, as if afraid that he had been heard.

I felt a moment of solidarity with him. He was my brother, after all. Maybe it was only Nephi who wasn't capable of feeling doubt. But I'd promised God that I would follow Father. Not Nephi, but Father. And for now, that seemed to me continuing into the desert. It wasn't what I wanted, either, but I couldn't forget my experience in the sandstorm so quickly.

"I don't know what God thinks," I said.

"Couldn't we ask God to go home?" asked Sam quietly. "Would that be a terrible thing to ask? If the people in Jerusalem are wicked, why can't God destroy just them and leave us?"

I didn't know the answer to Sam's question. He was only fifteen years old, so I felt sorry for him. Nephi was younger than he was by a year, but Nephi was the one who always told him what to do. Sam seemed younger in many ways.

Early on, Nephi had been the one Father decided was the epitome of all that was good in the world. He was obedient, quick to learn, and he rarely laughed about anything. I don't know why that was supposed to be such a good thing, but Father seemed to think it was. Nephi was deadly serious about everything, and whatever Father believed about God, multiply it by ten and that's what Nephi believed.

"I don't think God would listen to me," I said. "Even if I asked." Loving me wasn't the same as listening to me.

"Yeah," said Sam glumly. "I don't think He'd listen to me, either. Nephi says that's because I'm not asking for righteous things. I'm asking selfishly instead of telling God that I will do whatever I'm asked to do."

I guess God had His own ideas about which one of us was the easiest to work with, but Nephi had a lot to learn when it came to dealing with his older brothers.

"Maybe we'll start to like sand," I said, grinning at Sam and thinking that maybe he wasn't so bad, after all. I'd always assumed he was just like Nephi.

"I don't think that's possible." He gritted his teeth and made his hands into fists. "I'll always hate sand and I'll always wish that we could go back home." He looked toward the city we could no longer see, but I didn't want him to start thinking about heading back there in the middle of the night the way that Lemuel and I had. Clearly, that had been a bad plan.

"Sand has certain good qualities," I said.

"Like what?" He looked back at me, confused.

I grinned. "It's great for throwing," I said.

After that, Sam and I had a huge sand fight, throwing sand in each other's faces, down each other's backs, holding each other's heads in the sand until we nearly passed out, and then just lying back on the warm sand and staring at the hot sun overhead. It was the kind of thing Lemuel and I had been doing for years, but I'd never experienced with Sam. Maybe he wasn't as bad as I'd thought.

"Do you ever wonder what it would be like, if Nephi hadn't been born?" asked Sam after we'd been lying there in the sand a while. We were learning that you didn't move when it was this hot. You just waited until it was cool again, slept when you could, and used as little energy as possible.

I was surprised Sam was asking this question, but I guess he'd have been the prized youngest son without Nephi.

"Yeah, I think about that," I said. The truth was, I thought about it a lot.

"Maybe I'd be like Nephi, then," said Sam. "More like him," he added after a moment.

Maybe he would be, but this moment between us seemed to speak against that. I couldn't imagine having a sand fight with Nephi. "We don't talk very much," I said. "Maybe being in the desert will help change that." Maybe it was the one good thing about being here.

"You mean because there's not much else to do out here?"

"Well, besides looking for food and water," I said. "Yeah."

"We don't have nearly as much time for listening to scriptures," said Sam. "And Father didn't bring his scrolls."

"I'm so sorry about that part," I said sarcastically.

"He never made you listen to him," Sam pointed out.

"Because I was too big for him to make me do it," I said. "And you're too big for him to make you do it now, if you don't want to."

Sam thought about that for a while. "Sometimes I wish I didn't believe in God. But I do."

"Yeah, I know what you mean." I did now, anyway. After what had happened in the desert, I didn't doubt that God was real.

But then Nephi called to Sam in that authoritative voice he has, and Sam scampered up the banks to help put their things inside the tent once more.

Lemuel came to help me make my way back to the tent.

"What happened with you and Sam? Was that a fight you were having or just a game?"

"Mostly a game," I said.

"Did Sam tell you everything you were doing wrong while you did it?" asked Lemuel skeptically.

It was what I would have thought would happen, too. But it hadn't. "Actually, Sam is a pretty good guy. I think he's more like us than he wants to be."

Lemuel laughed at that.

"I mean it," I said. I explained what Sam had said about Nephi not being born and about wishing that he didn't believe in God.

"If we were still in Jerusalem, you know we wouldn't have any idea what was coming. We could enjoy ourselves without worrying about the future at all," said Lemuel.

"And then we'd die," I said. Was that what I really wanted? I realized that I had come to actually believe that Father was right about the fate of Jerusalem. When had that happened?

"But we'd die happy," said Lemuel. "With plenty of good food and wine in our stomachs."

"Do you ever wish that we'd been the ones born later?" I asked suddenly.

"What do you mean?"

I let out a long breath. "I mean, do you ever wish that we were Nephi and Sam instead of ourselves?" Did they feel the love of God all the time? It seemed unfair when I'd only felt it once in my life.

"Why would I wish that? They're so tightly wrapped I don't think they can breathe," said Lemuel.

"I know, but they seem so certain about everything. At least, Nephi does." And if he really did see Father's visions in his dreams at night, that seemed like it would be a good thing. Then we wouldn't be out here all this time wondering why we were here. We'd have purpose. We'd be self-righteous and annoying, but we'd know what we were doing and why. We'd believe in ourselves.

"If we were them, would they be us?" asked Lemuel.

"I don't know. I guess."

"Well, then, maybe I would wish for that sometimes. So they could know what Father was like when we were younger."

"And we'd know what Father was like now," I said.

"We already know what he's like now. We see him all the time, pretending to be a prophet when all he is, is an ordinary man," said Lemuel.

Was he just pretending? I didn't want to follow him, but it seemed clear to me that God had spoken to him about waiting for us when we were lost in the sandstorm. I didn't know why God chose certain people to be prophets and not others. Maybe he had to pick the crazy ones because no one else was willing to take the same risks. Maybe God had warned others about the end of Jerusalem and our father was the only one who was willing to leave everything behind and listen.

"What if we're the problem? What if he is a prophet and we don't want to see if because we got used to him the other way?" I asked.

Lemuel snorted at that.

Yeah, I knew that attitude, too. But it was too easy to fall back on, considering what we'd experienced. "You can't forget what happened in the sandstorm," I said.

Lemuel hesitated, then sighed. "Just because God saved us there, it doesn't mean that Father is a prophet."

Didn't it?

If I were God, maybe I would be more likely to talk to Father—and to Nephi. If I knew they were the ones who would listen to me and would never doubt. It didn't make me like my youngest brother more, though.

That night, when we stopped to make camp, no one found any animals to kill for dinner. Nephi suggested that the sandstorm had frightened them all away, and then had stared at me. As if it was my fault that the sandstorm had come in the first place.

"Good," I said. "I think I'm just fine without bloody, reeking, feathery meat that is half-cooked." I put a hand to my stomach, which was still sore after drinking too much water. Nephi was terrible at hunting and Mother was terrible at preparing meat for cooking. She'd let Lemuel and I do that when we were really poor and had let servants do it since Father came back.

Nephi stood close to me and shook a finger in my face. "You need to repent," he said. "You and Lemuel are the reason that we have been punished thusly."

Did he think he was going to intimidate me? My younger brother who was just barely as tall as I was? "Oh, really? You don't think it might just be because the desert is well—a desert?" I said sarcastically, giving him a chance to back down. "And that most of the animals tend to stay in places where there is more food and water?"

He didn't step back or lower his head. Some part of me knew why he was doing this. He had to prove himself to himself. And to Father.

"We have found water," said Nephi, waving a hand toward the stream we'd stumbled across, no thanks to him. "There should be may animals and birds here. But God has sent them away from us because we have not shown him proper thanks. We need to pour out our whole hearts to him and show our faith. We will not survive the wilderness if we do not rely upon Him completely."

Yes, I knew that he was the most faithful one of us. I knew that God—and Father—loved him best. But could he lord it over us a little less?

"Fine. You want me to pray and give thanks. I will." I threw up my arms and knelt down into the sand. "Thank you, God, for bringing us to water so that we can live." I had already said far more earnest thanks in my heart the night before, but if Nephi thought we had to pray out loud, fine.

I stood back up. I admit, I had felt nothing when I had prayed, not one moment of connection between me and God. Maybe I only felt that when I was in danger and I was really afraid. Maybe there was something wrong with me because of my childhood, when I had worried about everything every minute of the day. I don't know.

"You must pray with sincerity," said Nephi in that tone of voice that sounded like Father when he was reading from his scrolls and speaking as God Himself. "Trusting in the Lord in everything. You must show your love for Him in every word and every deed."

There was no lightning from heaven to strike Nephi down for blasphemy. Of course not. God approved of everything he did. And nothing I did was good enough for Nephi.

I could talk to Sam. He was a regular person, with flaws and weaknesses. But Nephi? He was way above me. I guess that was why God could speak to him and not to me. They were closer to the same clouds.

"You could use that bow and arrow to shoot me," I suggested. "And then the rest of the party wouldn't be punished for my wickedness." I flung out my arms and waited for him to do something. If he didn't want to use the bow and arrow, he could just hit me.

There was almost nothing I wanted more at that moment than the chance to fight Nephi physically. Oh, I didn't think that I would win necessarily. He was very strong, and he had youth on his side. And certainty.

But at least I would have a better chance measuring myself against him that way than in the way that he was constantly measuring me spiritually. And there would be the satisfaction of the physical fight itself. I thought that the grunting and the pressure of muscle against muscle could be enormously therapeutic. I was angry at Nephi, and this would be one way to let that anger out.

"I will not hurt you," Nephi said, holding out his hands and letting them drop to his sides after a moment.

Then he walked away and spoke to Father and Mother quietly in their tents. Everyone stared at me as if it was my fault our stomachs were all grumbling.

I had all this pent up energy from Nephi's refusal, so I had to wrestle with Lemuel that night instead. I noticed Sam came over and watched us that night as we pinned each other again and again. I gave as good as I got. Lemuel and I were very evenly matched, and I think we knew each other too well to fool anyone by our "moves." We also fought dirty, no gentleman's rules. No tapping out to say you were finished, you were giving up before you got really hurt.

By the end, we were both bloody, exhausted, and sore. We'd be more sore in the morning. But somehow, I felt happier, lighter, as if fighting had relieved a burden of mine. If Nephi understood me better, he would have seen how fighting with me would have been a gift. But sometimes you have to get what you need from people who really understand you. Nephi would never be that.

In the morning, we broke camp and kept close to the river for the rest of the day. To my surprise, Nephi found some roots growing by the bank that Mother managed not to burn. No animals still, but at least there was something to put in my belly to keep it from feeling so hollow.

I had no idea if God had decided that He wasn't punishing us anymore or not. I had thought about God as I fell asleep the night before, but I did not know how to pray properly. I couldn't put real feeling in it. I liked to blame that on Father's lack of teaching, but maybe it was me, after all.

I listened as Nephi gave a long prayer to God, thanking Him for His mercy in showing where to find food.

I tried to feel grateful. We were alive. We had found water, which was the most important thing. Lemuel and I had survived that terrible sandstorm. We were supposed to survive the ransacking and pillaging of Jerusalem that was coming.

But mostly, I just felt hungry.

I looked at Sam and saw him on his knees, spitting sand out of his mouth. Apparently he'd tried to eat it to keep his stomach from being empty. Stupid, but the kind of thing you expect a kid to do. He looked utterly miserable.

I went over and invited him to come and walk with me and Lemuel. He took a long moment to consider the offer, then looked at Nephi and shook his head at me.

I didn't blame him, not really. He had to make a choice, and he'd chosen the side that looked like it was going to win.

The next day, we followed the stream until it was met by several others and turned into a river which flowed into a beautiful valley with no sand at all, but real dirt, rich and ready for planting.

Father began to sing and dance as he walked along next to Mother, tickling her and making her laugh. She seemed younger than she had been for many years, and I began to see how taking her away from Jerusalem had been a good thing, after all. In the city, she had always had so much to do, to worry about, to compare herself to.

After we camped for the evening, and while it was still light, Nephi managed to use his bow and arrow to kill several birds. So I suppose we were forgiven for whatever sins we had committed at last.

Mother had gotten better at preparing the birds for cooking, neatly and quickly taking off feathers and scooping out the guts.

Sam and Lemuel were in charge of the fire, and Lemuel warned Nephi off until the fire was mostly hot coals, so the food would cook more slowly and evenly. At least Nephi would let Lemuel do something that was useful. I stayed away because I was sure Nephi would think I was cursed and would ruin anything I touched.

The meat was perfectly roasted and tasted all the better because we were so hungry. We all feasted while it was still light out, and as it grew dark, Father built an altar of stones and gave thanks to God.

I felt thankful even if I didn't say any prayer of my own. Perhaps one day I would learn to hear God's voice as easily as Father did. It might change my life. I might be just as crazy as Father was. I smiled at the thought, and was about to drift to sleep when Father said my name.

"Laman, I name this river after you which flows into the Red Sea. And I pray that thou mightiest be like unto this river, continually running into the fountain of all righteousness."

It ruined all my sense of peace and pleasure in this place. My gratitude felt stripped from me because Father had to point out again how I was falling short.

Then Father said, "And you, Lemuel. I name this valley after you, this place of our respite and relief. O that thou mightest be like unto this valley, firm and steadfast, and immovable in keeping the commandments of the Lord."

I waited for a long moment, expecting Father to say a prayer for Nephi or Sam, or possibly for Mother. He could name other things after them. The trees, or the plants around us. The stars that were beginning to wink out over our heads. The wind, the weeds, the bugs that were starting to bite us, anything at all. But no, Lemuel and I were unique. Only we needed to be prayed over. Because there was so much wrong with us.

Lemuel and I went to bed in our own tents, and I listened to the sound of the river for a long time before I fell asleep.

9

The next day, Father woke us all early. "I have an important announcement to make. It is about returning to Jerusalem. Rise and dress and come to the fire for a family meeting."

Returning to Jerusalem? I sighed relief at this, sure that we had passed whatever test that God had invented for us. Father must have had a dream or a vision or heard a voice telling him that it was acceptable. Now we could go back to living in our nice, comfortable home. We could work on giving more to the poor. We could help Father with his message of repentance to the people. And we'd save Jerusalem from whatever terrible fate might have happened without us.

Lemuel and I dressed and went out to the circle that had Father at its center. Nephi was already there. Of course he was. Father would have told him first. Or God would have.

I looked at the sky and took a breath and told myself that this was the answer to my prayers, too, even if I didn't deserve to have them answered. Then I looked around at our family again, and thought about how lucky we all were. We were still alive. We were still together. That was enough to rejoice in, surely.

Lemuel sat next to me, gripping my hand firmly. I stared at Nephi, who seemed unusually quiet and stoic. I admit, I thought that Nephi would learn a lesson about

Father now. Nephi might have believed we would go to a Promised Land, but he overestimated Father's strength.

In the end, I was the one who learned the lesson. About Father, about Nephi, and about myself.

"Nephi and Sam and Laman and Lemuel, you are to go to the house of Laban and ask him to give you the Plates of Brass. God has commanded us that we should have the records of our people in the Promised Land. Without them, our descendants will not know of the stories of God's dealings with His children. They will not know the law. And they will lose the language that binds them to their ancestors."

I wanted to roll my eyes. Of course, Father had realized now that we had been in the wilderness three days that he had nothing to do out here without his scriptures. He had no way of making Nephi and Sam sit at his feet and listen to him pontificate. How could he make himself look important and knowledgeable if we didn't have some ancient writings for him to read and explain to them?

"Did God actually tell you to send us to go get these plates?" I asked. Or had Father just decided that this was what he needed? It seemed awfully easy to me for Father to translate what God supposedly wanted into what he wanted, and make it all into a dream.

"Of course He did. How can you doubt that?" said Father, his face suffusing with red. "I am His prophet and He spoke to me clearly in the night."

"Fine. Did He send some instruction along, as well, then? Did He tell us where to steal them from? Give us the code that will get us into the special place that our cousin Laban is keeping them?" I asked.

Nephi stood up and moved to Father's side. "I believe that Father heard these commands from God," he said.

Nephi was all ready to go wherever Father told him to go. He wanted those scriptures as much as Father did, because he needed a purpose, too. He needed to feel that he was the special one who knew more than the rest of us, and was not just handier with a bow and arrow in the wilderness.

"God does not command us in all things," said Father. "You will have to find your own answers to the question of how to do what He has laid out for you. You will learn a great deal about yourselves, I think, and about how to work with each other."

I seriously wondered if Father had misunderstood. Maybe we could go back to Jerusalem and get something else. Like coins we could use with passing traders. Or more food. Possibly some nicer furniture to put in our tents and to sleep on, if we were going to be out here for a long time.

I looked at Lemuel and I could see he was thinking the same thing. Father was conveniently sending us back into the city instead of going himself. My guess was that he was tired and was nervous about making it back that far in terms of physical strength and endurance. Maybe he was afraid that Mother and Sam would refuse to keep going once they realized how bad it would be. Nephi I think he was more sure of.

Or maybe he thought that if he tried to go back himself, the people in the city would recognize him and stone him for what he'd said to them. Or just laugh at him until he stopped talking about his dreams from God and just decided to stay where life was comfortable and easy and forget about God's visions and dreams.

Whatever the reason, I told myself that Lemuel and I could bring back with us a few more provisions. More bows and arrows. Skins for water. Spices for the meat we were going to have to eat out here. Maybe some seeds.

I didn't care about the Plates of Brass in the least. I cared about surviving. And if Father said that God wanted us to figure things out on our own, then why not figure out that? We didn't have to depend on God for everything at every moment of our lives, did we?

If we stayed in this valley, I bet we could grow things here quite well. We could live here, in fact, maybe convince Father this was the Promised Land. And it wasn't so far from Jerusalem that we couldn't go back now and again, if we wanted to. Convince some women to come back with us, since it was going to be awfully lonely out here. I didn't know what kind of women would be willing to come back with us, but we couldn't be picky, could we?

Nephi stood and spoke loudly and firmly: "I will go and do the things which the Lord hath commanded, for I know that the Lord giveth no commandment unto the children of men save He shall prepare a way for them to accomplish the thing which He commandeth them."

Sam was looking up at Nephi in awe. Lemuel rolled his eyes.

I was thinking again striking Nephi across the face. Would he fight back then? Or would he just stand there and take it, quoting scriptures at me the whole while and calling me to repentance? No wonder Father was staying away from Jerusalem.

But Father embraced Nephi and wept upon his shoulder. He called him "beloved son" and then told him that God would bless him exceedingly for this in the Promised Land, and that he would be the leader of his brothers, in this and many other things.

I glanced over at Lemuel and could see he was at least as angry as I was. It was one thing for Father to weep over Nephi being such a good son. I was used to that. But telling him that he was going to be the leader of this expedition? That wasn't the way it was supposed to be. I was the eldest. And besides, I knew the city a lot better than Nephi did. I was pretty sure I had a much better chance of convincing Laban of anything than he did. And whatever Father said, I was not going to follow Nephi's orders.

Father saw no reason for us to delay and patted Nephi on the back, preparing to say goodbye to him.

I tried to think of an excuse to stay for a little longer, mostly because my contrary nature didn't want to obey Father so quickly. But what reason did I have to stay here in the desert?

It was not a celebratory departure. Mother wept, and when Father tried to console her, she turned her back on him, went into the tent and closed the flap on him. I wanted to cheer for her on that point, but instead Lemuel and I just gave each other fist bumps.

Go, Mother! She'd been pretty feisty back in the days when Father wasn't around, and she had to be, to protect herself and us. Maybe she'd be like that again out here in the desert.

I thought Sam would be a little puppy dog around Nephi, but he didn't seem very happy about crossing back over the desert and back into Jerusalem. I could see that he was watching Lemuel and me to see if we could figure out a way to make Nephi go back as we headed away. We were leaving all the animals with Father. Good choice, that. Because if we didn't make it back, Father and Mother could still have a shot of making it back to Jerusalem before they died of starvation.

The first night in the desert, I made sure that Lemuel and I shared guard duty overnight. Nephi didn't even think about it. He was so certain that his God would watch over him that he went right to sleep, wrapped in nothing more than a thin blanket.

I couldn't help but wonder what would happen if God forgot about us? What if He let His attention slip for one moment and then some marauders came and killed us for sport or animals came and devoured us or a scorpion came along and stung us all four in a row? Was God going to go to the trouble of saving us in that case? Or would He just find another family He could get to leave Jerusalem and head out into the wilderness to do whatever it was that we were supposed to do?

I didn't get much sleep, and I didn't care. I didn't even wake up Lemuel when he nodded off.

In the morning, Nephi seemed to have a panic attack as he realized that there was nothing to eat and no way to catch it since we'd left our weapons with Father.

When Sam went over to try to get Nephi started packing up, Nephi had a little tantrum, shouting and throwing himself on the ground.

After that, Sam came over and sat by me and Lemuel.

Eventually, Nephi got to his knees and started praying. I don't know what he said or what he heard. I was just annoyed that we were sitting around in the worst heat of the desert sun.

Nephi would never go back to Father alone and admit he had failed. I knew that much about him. He'd just wander in the desert and die. Or he'd find his way to Jerusalem and figure out how to get the Plates on his own, get back to Father days before we did, and then maybe Father would move on without us. Or scold us for being so lazy and late when we arrived.

Somehow Nephi would get all of the rest of us in trouble. It was a gift that he had.

So we just waited for him to calm down and focus. I was sure he was afraid of facing Laban. By all accounts, Laban wasn't a nice guy. He earned a lot of money from his position, which wasn't strictly ethical. But even apart from that, he was known to be a bad enemy to have. Like fatally bad. Laban had goons all over the city who either belonged to him or owed him favors. We weren't going to be able to just walk in and ask for a favor and Nephi knew it.

He spent all day praying, without food or water, suffering in the desert sun. But in the end, he didn't get an answer that got him off the hook.

That evening, Nephi came over and said what Lemuel and I could have told him already if he'd asked us. "We must walk through the night. We have to move away from the water and we must be careful not to sweat too much in the sun. "

Lemuel and I just nodded to him that we understood. If we'd tried to speak, we would have laughed at him, but Father had told us he was in charge. So let him be in charge and take the blame when none of this worked.

Walking at night, it took us four days to get back to the outskirts of Jerusalem. Lemuel and I became quite good at nodding quietly to whatever Nephi said, and at ignoring the increasing hunger and thirst we felt. If we all died, well it would be Nephi's fault. At least Father wouldn't think so highly of him anymore. And Mother would cry over us when they found our bodies.

Sam woke up every evening and got out of the tent he shared with Nephi. He looked unhappy, and like he'd have preferred to share space with me and Lemuel. But he didn't ask. He didn't say anything against Nephi. He looked like he was preparing for death and praying to God for it to come quickly.

Each night as we walked in the darkness, I thought about when Lemuel and I had tried to return to Jerusalem. Why couldn't God have told us that we had to get the Brass Plates from Laban? Why did He send us back to bring Nephi with us? Was it really that God thought Nephi was the best of the four brothers? Was Nephi learning how to rule over us, the way God intended for it to be in the future?

I didn't pray. I didn't ask God for a sign. I was afraid that He would show me precisely what I didn't want to see, that Nephi was supposed to be in charge because God thought only Nephi could do this. I hated Nephi, though I knew I shouldn't. Was it his fault that God had chosen him or was it mine?

10

As the dawn rose, Nephi looked at the city on the horizon as if he was astonished to see the buildings still standing, exactly as they had been when we left.

"Not destroyed yet," I said cheerfully.

"It will be," Nephi promised darkly.

"Well, most cities are destroyed. And rebuilt. And destroyed again. It's the way of life. There is no life without the cycle of death," I said, thinking that sounded pretty wise.

I was the older brother. There were really some things that Nephi hadn't seen yet. He was just a kid. When I had been his age—well, I really never had been his age. I had never been allowed to be that naïve.

For just a moment, looking at him, despite my anger at God, I felt a wave of protectiveness. He was my younger brother. He was a pain a lot of the time. He got way more attention than was good for him. He was naive and unworldly. But he was my flesh and blood.

"We should go and see Laban immediately!" Nephi announced. His hands were clenched into fists and I was pretty sure I understood his thought process. He had always been the kind of kid who ate his vegetables first and saved his favorite food, the nuts, for last. He wanted to get this confrontation over with, and then he could relax again.

The rest of us had other ideas, however.

"What? We just got out of the desert. Let's find something to drink first," said Sam.

"And eat," Lemuel added.

"And rest," I said, because Laban was not going to be easy to deal with. Putting on some nicer clothes that didn't smell like they'd been in the desert for weeks and that made us look like we had something valuable to bargain with couldn't hurt, either.

But you can't talk sense to some people, and Nephi was one of them.

So I let him go. I went with him, but I didn't do anything on my own. I was there to watch. And learn what not to do. I admit, I was sort of looking forward to watching him fail. He was supposed to be in charge of this whole thing. He was going to report to Father on what he had done, so let him.

Dressed like nomad tribes or like crazy people, we went to Laban's house and asked politely for entry.

I could tell the servants were laughing at us behind their sleeves even if Nephi didn't notice. If they felt at all sorry for us, they would have warned us or sent us away and told us to come back later. But I think that Laban was already in a bad mood that day, and they probably figured that they might as well let him take out his bad mood on us as on them.

Nephi stood in front of all of us and addressed Laban in formal words.

"My father has been commanded by God to leave Jerusalem because it will be destroyed due to its wickedness. God will lead us to a new Promised Land where we will raise up righteous posterity unto Him, and we would become a new Jerusalem."

"What is this supposed to mean?" demanded Laban. He looked like he was ready to kill someone with his bare hands.

"We must have the Plates of Brass so that we can teach our children in the language of our fathers, so that they will have the records of God's dealings with His children in times of old. Without this, they might forget Him and His ways and dwindle in unbelief," Nephi went on.

"You're asking for the Plates of Brass?" said Laban, waving a hand impatiently. "Is that it?"

"God is asking for them, yes," said Nephi.

"Is God going to pay for them?" asked Laban.

"My father had a dream," said Nephi. He was starting to lose his confidence. His hands were shaking. I was pretty sure I had never seen Nephi this frightened or out of his depth before. His whole life, Father had trained him in every little thing before he expected Nephi to do anything on his own.

I felt a little pity for him, and a lot of amusement.

I wasn't going to let Laban kill my younger brother, but if he beat him a bit, I could see how that might actually turn out for our good. If God wanted Nephi to learn to be a leader, maybe some humility would help us all follow him more happily.

"The Brass Plates are my inheritance. My father had them, and his father before him, back generations. The prophets themselves wrote upon those plates and they have been entrusted to my family, who has protected them all these many years," said Laban.

"Yes, but Jerusalem is to be destroyed. My father saw it in a dream," said Nephi. "We cannot allow the Brass Plates to be destroyed—or possibly taken by the invaders, whoever they are."

He sounded insane. Just like Father sounded insane when he preached in the streets the last few months before we left.

"Oh, so you're just going to take care of the Brass Plates, is that it?" said Laban. His eyes were gleaming. He wasn't pleased. He wasn't interested in what Nephi was saying at all. He was just toying with him.

"Yes. And read them to our children and our children's children," said Nephi piously.

"Because your children and their children deserve to have the teachings on these Brass Plates. But my children and my children's children do not," said Laban blandly.

"Uh," said Nephi. He had realized at last that Laban was not happy and that he was in danger of Laban's anger.

"I had heard that your father had not been seen in some days. Is he dead?" asked Laban.

"N—no," said Nephi. He seemed to have developed a stutter, which made me think about Moses, whom Nephi admired so much. Maybe God had answered a prayer of Nephi's with this twisted sense of humor, making him more like the prophet he admired than Nephi had ever wished he would be.

"He is living, but he sent you to ask for the Brass Plates? His youngest son? And why is that?" asked Laban. He glanced at me and Lemuel. He must have known who we were, that we were the elder sons, but he'd never spoken to us.

"Our father trusts me because he knows that I am obedient to the commands of the Lord," said Nephi, looking at me. But what was I supposed to do to help him now? If he'd asked before we got here, I would have given him some hints, but it was sink or swim for him now. All on his own.

Laban looked like a spider contemplating an insect before deciding if it was worth catching it and putting it in its web. "I see. He sent you to ask me to give you my most prized possession. And in exchange for this, he offered no compensation at all. I thought your father was a businessman."

"They will be of no use to you," said Nephi. "When—" he stopped as he realized that Laban didn't believe our father's dream about Jerusalem being destroyed.

Laban said, "If your father wants the Brass Plates, he must come to me himself. Not send his youngest son as only a coward would do."

I tried to wave Nephi to silence, but he ignored me.

"I must do as God commands," he said. "I must get the Brass Plates and bring them into the wilderness."

"Into the wilderness? Because that's where God would want the Brass Plates to be? All that knowledge, all that history, and God would want it to be in the desert with a drunken, madman and his dubious sons?"

That was precisely how most people in Jerusalem thought of Father. Drunk and mad. And I wasn't sure that him being here would have helped dispel that impression, either. But Nephi believed in him so much. I couldn't have pulled off this act. I didn't have the faith. Maybe that was why he had to be the leader.

"We will be led to a new Promised Land. We will create a new civilization!" said Nephi proudly.

Laban simply laughed aloud at him. "Go now, and save your life. I do not take pleasure in killing little boys. Even boys as ill-mannered as yourself." He waved a hand at the door, which was suddenly opened. There were guards all around us, holding spears and swords up to our throats. There was not much choice in the matter of leaving.

By the time we were thrown sprawling into the street, I was simply glad that we had survived the ordeal. Laban had shown us mercy, as far as I was concerned. He was right about being the proper keeper of the Brass Plates. Father should never have asked us to come like this. He should have come himself before he left Jerusalem. If he really had been guided by God, then why had he made such a terrible mistake?

"Let's go home," said Lemuel. "I'm tired and I want to sleep in a real bed for a little while."

Was he admitting that we'd be heading back into the wilderness? It was hard for me to imagine going back now. It was one thing when Father announced it so suddenly. But he wasn't here now. And the wilderness seemed so far away. It was so much more comfortable here.

"We can stay in our house, can't we, Nephi?" asked Sam. "For today. Until we decide what to do next."

What was there to do next? We'd asked Laban for the Plates. He'd given us a resounding answer. I couldn't see what else Father could expect us to do. Laban's house was filled with guards. Even if we wanted to try to break in and steal the Plates, there was no way that we could succeed. And now that Nephi had done what he had done, Laban was likely to be even more careful about guarding them.

"God said that we would get the Plates," said Nephi. He seemed smaller and younger than ever.

"Well, maybe God gets things wrong sometimes," I said. I just didn't want to be in the streets any longer. We looked like beggars, and I'd already seen people passing us. Would they call the city guard to throw us out? Going home seemed like the best idea to me. We could go there, think about what would be useful to bring back with us. Then go tell Father it didn't work.

"God can't get things wrong," said Nephi. "He is God."

"Well, maybe Father got it wrong, then," said Lemuel. "He heard it wrong or something."

"Or maybe God wanted us to come and try, but He didn't expect us to succeed," said Sam.

"No," said Nephi. "God promised me that I would succeed. But I don't understand how. I had faith and courage. And still Laban refused me."

Wouldn't it be nice to live in a world where faith and courage were all that was required to get what you wanted? Poor, naïve Nephi. There was more than one way for God to teach a lesson.

"We'll try again tomorrow," I suggested. "After going home and dressing properly. After all, wasn't Moses told to take off his shoes before he spoke to God? Aren't we commanded to clean ourselves and dress in our best before we bring offerings to the temple?"

Nephi brightened at this. "Yes. I should have thought of that! Of course, you're right, Laman. I should have listened to you. You are my elder brother. Father must have sent you with me for a reason, so that you could give me advice."

How nice that he acknowledged I might have some value beyond just carrying a bag for him.

"I say we drink ourselves blind tonight," said Lemuel in my ear. "And Nephi can do whatever he wants tomorrow."

I smirked at him, but in my heart, I was worried. Nephi was going to come back to Laban soon, and Laban was not going to treat him kindly the second time. If we didn't go with him, would he be in danger? If Nephi was killed, we couldn't go back to Father in the wilderness and tell him. We would have to stay here. Which should have sounded like a great idea.

So why didn't it?

"Nephi?" I asked.

"I don't know what to do," he said dejectedly.

"We'll just take a rest and you can pray. Maybe God will send you a dream about what to do next," I said, and took his arm.

He was dejected enough that he let me guide him through the streets and back to our home. A good night's sleep would be good for all of us.

The house was still standing, just as we had left it. There had been no looting, and I suspected from the lack of dust that the servants had been coming in to clean despite the fact that Father told them we would not be coming back. They must have decided he would change his mind. Maybe he would.

I tucked Nephi into his bed as if he were a small child again. He whimpered a little in his sleep and I patted him, fearing to leave his side. I eventually curled up in a blanket on the floor next to him, feeling like his elder brother for the first time in a great many years.

We slept all that day and all that night, the sleep of the righteous and weary.

But in the morning, when Nephi woke, he was transformed into his old self once more, as certain as ever. God, he claimed, had sent him his own dream and in it had told him how he would get the Plates.

11

"God told me that we must gather up all our most precious things from our house and give them to Laban in exchange for the Plates of Brass. Laban is well known as an astute businessman, isn't he, Laman? That was what I saw in the dream. He will see our wealth and he will desire it. Then he will give us the Plates and we will go back to Father, having obeyed his command." Nephi was practically bouncing with excitement.

I admit that I was suffering from a significant hangover. Lemuel and I hadn't had a drink in over a week, and the temptation to give in to finishing off the store left in the house was too much. We weren't going to have the chance to drink for the next several years—or more.

I groaned and held my head, wishing that the servants were still here and would bring me one of those concoctions they used to offer us when we woke up after a late night drinking.

My mouth tasted foul and it was filled with gunk that made it nearly impossible to speak. I glanced around the room for Sam and couldn't find him for a moment. I panicked, wondering what Father would say to us if we returned without Sam. I hopped around the room and finally found him in a corner.

I nudged him awake and let Nephi repeat his dream.

Sam hadn't had as much to drink as Lemuel and I had, but he was also not used to it, so I think it may have affected him even worse. He vomited several times and then started nodding to everything Nephi said. Mostly to get him to quit talking, I think.

Why couldn't he just give us until the end of the day? We had just come back from a stressful trip into the desert where we had nearly starved to death.

"Come on. Let's get going. I'll go out and get a wagon to come to the house and we can load it with everything. You three stay in here and start making a collection of the best things. Gold, silver, anything Father traded in. One of a kind items. Silks, satins, rugs, scrolls, that kind of thing," said Nephi imperiously. He was really taking this in charge thing seriously now.

I was tempted to send Nephi off for the wagon and just fall back to sleep. Or find some water to wash my mouth out with. Then I could deal with him later by telling him that we were not going to do this, not now and not tomorrow, either.

"Sam, you have that gold goblet, don't you?" said Nephi. "Didn't Father give you that when you turned ten?"

"Ung," he said.

"I'm not going to give Laban anything," said Lemuel, holding out his hands in defense. "That's the stupidest idea I ever heard."

"Why?" said Nephi. "It's a good deal for all of us. We don't need any of the stuff here in the house. I think God must have sent angels to watch over it to make sure that nothing was stolen while we were gone. He must intend for us to use it for this purpose. Why else would it still be here, just as before?"

Maybe because people were afraid that if they came in here, they would be afflicted with the same disease that

Father had, that made him go crazy, leave all his precious possessions and take his family into the wilderness to die?

"But the Brass Plates aren't worth nearly that much. They're just brass, after all," said Lemuel. He was still reasoning with Nephi as if anything he'd said were remotely rational. It was the same as with Father, when he was talking about his dream. He'd gone into a different realm of thinking and feeling.

"They're the history of our ancestors' dealings with God. They have the words of the prophets on them," said Nephi with that far-away tone of religious authority. "They're far more valuable than anything we have in this house."

Lemuel glanced over and smirked at me at this. "Then why would Laban trade them for gold?" he asked.

Nephi paused a moment to think about that. In that moment, I had a brief hope that he would really think and be rational. But of course, he wasn't.

"Because Laban is an evil man, a selfish and greedy man. He doesn't intend to follow the commandments of God. That's not why he wants the Brass Plates. He wants them only because they have a monetary value, and we can compensate him for those," Nephi said.

"He hates us!" Sam put in. "He won't give us anything if he can help it."

That was definitely true. Points to Sam.

"But he loves money," said Nephi.

"He hates us more," said Sam. "And he's a scary guy. I don't think we should go back there. Ever."

Why had I ever said anything against Sam? Clearly, he was the younger brother that I'd always wanted.

"God says that we should go. That means that we should go," said Nephi stolidly.

"What if he takes everything and still won't give us the Brass Plates?" said Sam.

I wanted to clap for him. That was an excellent question.

Which meant that Nephi refused to answer it. "God told me that this is the way to get the Brass Plates. I will follow Him. I know that He will provide a way for us to obey Him. So long as we are willing to sacrifice sufficiently."

Was it a sacrifice to Nephi to give up all of this? Probably not as much as it was for the rest of us. Nephi had grown up rich and I think that meant that he didn't notice wealth as much as the rest of us did. Even Sam had spent a little bit of time before Father had gotten truly wealthy. He might not know what it was like to be hungry, but he knew how much he liked it when we had moved to a bigger house and had more servants and better food. He knew the difference between people ignoring him and people staring at him in awe because of the clothes he wore.

It was a strange thing about Nephi that he was so unaware of how much those things mattered. He had spent that time in the desert hungry with the rest of us, but it hadn't penetrated. He hadn't grown up in fear of having no food, and I think in some part of his mind, he didn't believe it was possible. He didn't go to bed sure that he'd wake up hungry still. He went to bed with the optimism to believe that in the morning, it would all be fine again.

I didn't know if I should feel sorry for him or be angry with him for being so stupid about this. If we gave everything away, then there was no second option. We would have to stay in the desert because we would have no other options left. Whereas if we left everything in the house, and went and told Father we couldn't get the Brass Plates, maybe we could convince him to come home.

Wouldn't God want us to have a back-up in case we couldn't make it to the Promised Land? If God loved us, wouldn't He want us to be safe? After all, how long had Father spent thinking about this journey? We could have planned better. We could have taken years to map out the right routes, to make sure we had all the right tools. Perhaps a caravan of wagons, or a ship to meet us at the coast.

"We're not going to help you," said Lemuel, crossing his arms over his chest. "Nothing you say can change our minds."

"But—" said Nephi. He looked at me.

As if I was going to help him.

"Laman, Father told us to get the Brass Plates. We can't return without them."

"I know that," I said.

"God doesn't want us to stay here. Jerusalem could be destroyed at any moment. He wants us to be safe."

Is that what God wanted for us? Or did He just want to see if we would do whatever He told us to do? Would Nephi have jumped off a cliff if God told him to? Maybe he would.

"Jerusalem is not going to be destroyed. Not any time soon," said Lemuel. He waved a hand around. "You're making too much of a fuss over that."

"How do you know?" asked Nephi.

"You can tell such things. We're all prosperous. We have no enemies," said Lemuel.

"We need to go. Now. We cannot wait. We cannot allow our attachment to things of this world to overpower us," Nephi said urgently.

I stared at him and wondered if the reason he felt so urgent was that he just a little bit tempted to stay here, like I was. Was he trying to make sure that he couldn't come back? So that he had to obey God's commandments?

"You're crazy," said Lemuel. "Laman, tell him he's crazy."

"Nephi, you're crazy," I said easily. Was there any question about that? Our father was crazy, too. The problem was that crazy people got things done. Wasn't Moses crazy? He told Pharaoh to let his people go. Pharaoh laughed. And then Moses did a bunch of crazy things, until the craziest of all was the death of all the first born sons of all the Egyptians.

But the crazy didn't end there. Moses told his people to walk right into the Red Sea with him, to trust that the walls above them would stay there, that they would all live. And after that, Moses expected our ancestors to stay with him all those years in the wilderness, wandering when they knew the Promised Land wasn't that far away.

That was crazy. As far as I could tell, God used crazy people for His own purposes. Maybe that was the real reason that Lemuel and I didn't hear much from God. Maybe we weren't crazy enough to do the crazy things that He wanted done.

"How about we just give Laban some of it?" said Sam, trying to be the moderator. "That way we can try again doing something else."

Like what? I wanted to ask. Did Sam think we could hire someone to break into Laban's house with the rest of our money? Laban had a lot of guards. And a terrible temper. Unless the person breaking into the house was planning to leave Jerusalem directly afterward—and maybe join our group in the desert—I didn't think anyone would take us up on the offer. Laban would surely take his revenge and no amount of money would make up for being dead.

"We can't do it halfway. God expects a full sacrifice to prove ourselves to Him," said Nephi, channeling Father again with that booming voice in a super low register.

"I still don't see why we can't wait until tomorrow at least," Lemuel grumbled.

And after tomorrow, another tomorrow. Yeah, I knew how Lemuel was thinking.

"Sam, you'll help me, won't you?" said Nephi, turning to him.

Sam looked down at his feet. Poor Sam. Nephi knew just how to twist him to do what he wanted.

"I guess," Sam finally said.

"Good. I'll be back soon." Nephi turned.

"Wait!" I called out. "What if this still doesn't work? We need to think of a plan B." A plan C, really, but I didn't bring up the failure with Laban already. I thought it was nice of me, not that Nephi would notice.

Nephi turned back. "We must have absolute faith in God. He sent me a vision. He has shown us the way. We must follow Him. He loves us and He will always help us to do as He asks." He was so sure of this.

"God doesn't love me," I said softly. "Not like He loves you."

"God loves all His children. He sends more tests to those He thinks are capable of more."

"So you're saying I should take it as a compliment and a sign of His love that He's asking us to do the impossible?" I asked.

"It is not impossible with God," said Nephi.

That's what he thought. He just hadn't lived long enough to know how untrue that was. God sent us plenty of challenges He knew that we couldn't manage. He asked us to do things He knew were impossible because He wanted us to fail. At least, He'd wanted me and Lemuel to fail. But Nephi just couldn't conceive of failure. What a rude awakening he was going to have.

"And what then? If Laban refuses to give us the Brass Plates, we go back to Father in the wilderness?" I wanted a promise from him that he'd face up to the reality of Father's impossible command.

But of course, he didn't.

"God will not allow us to fail," he insisted. "If Laban refuses this, then we will think of another way. God will have another way waiting for us to find."

And another and another, apparently.

"But I believe Laban will trade the plates. His greed will be his undoing. And thus will God prove Himself the God of All by making his enemy show the truth of his weakness," said Nephi.

If he was trying to write scripture, it needed a few more revisions. That was my opinion, anyway.

"Fine. Then you can go take everything you can carry to Laban and ask him to give you the Brass Plates yourself," I said. I pointed to the rest of us. "We don't want to come with you."

I could see Sam was still wavering. He didn't know which side to be on.

"Alone?" asked Nephi.

"I thought you said that God would be with you. And that nothing was impossible with God."

Nephi was silent for a long moment. Then he said, "Sam?"

Sam, be strong! I whispered the words, but Sam bowed his head.

"I'll go with you, Nephi," he said.

"Lemuel?" said Nephi.

This was how Nephi defeated us, by attacking us one at a time.

Lemuel looked at me. "Laman?" he said.

Did I think that God really wanted us to have the Brass Plates? Yes, I did. He hadn't spoken to me, but then again, why should He? I wasn't crazy. I wouldn't do anything He asked of me like Nephi would. If I were God, I would want someone like Nephi to do my bidding, too, not someone like me who was cynical and selfish. I'd only bother with me if I got in the way.

"I'll come," I said with a sigh. I wasn't doing it for God, though. I was doing it for Nephi. He was my little brother, even if he was a pain. I needed to protect him because no one else would. It wasn't really about Father's expectations, after all. It was what I expected of myself.

"Thank you, Laman," said Nephi. "God will reward you for this, you know."

Would He? God had strange ways of rewarding people. Like Father, who had finally turned his life around. What was his reward for that? He got visions about the destruction of Jerusalem that might or might not come true in our lifetime. Father got to leave all his comforts, all his wealth, behind, and go live in a tent in the wilderness.

And all the people who hadn't been worthy to hear God speak to them? They got to stay here in Jerusalem for as long as it lasted. They got to enjoy life and have no idea of what was coming to them.

We hired a wagon and filled it with the most expensive things we could find: linens, swords, helmets, lamps, cushions, hangings. As well as coins of gold, silver, and brass.

I admit it, I was impressed with my younger brother. He could have done anything with his life. Really, most people find him personable. When he isn't talking about God, he knows how to lead people. He's handsome (more than I am, I admit—though the lack of scars on his face from being beaten by Father doesn't hurt). And he's strong enough he could have competed with anyone in Jerusalem and won. He could have had wealth and fame here. But he gave it up to follow Father. And Father's God.

Nephi drove the wagon to Laban's house just as it was getting dark. We arrived and Nephi carried as much as he could inside. He knocked on Laban's door as we stood behind him, carrying as much as we could, as well.

The noise inside was so raucous it took Nephi several rounds of knocking, despite his strength against that wood.

Finally, we were shown into a well-lit, incense-filled room. I noticed Nephi's look of disgust when he saw the gold idols that Laban had set up in the room. I had no idea if he worshipped them or if he just liked the look. Or the value. But it didn't set the right tone for the meeting.

Nephi had us all drop our packs and spread out everything on the floor, so that Laban could see it all.

Laban walked around the room, touching everything with a finger, sniffing at it if he wanted to. When he stopped by me, he nudged me with a fist. "Sunk this far, have you? Trailing after your younger brother like he's the eldest?"

It was just the thing to make me fume inside and Laban knew it.

"We bring you all of this in exchange for the Brass Plates. You can have what remains at our father's house, as well. It is more than a bargain for you," said Nephi imperiously.

He could really use some lessons on how to negotiate. For one thing, he hadn't offered a lower price and then tried to bargain his way to some middle zone. He'd set out everything and if Laban refused, we had no way to go up from here. Plus, we'd come without any servants or guards, and Laban had dozens of men in the room with him, not to mention a legion of guards within his call.

I had a bad feeling even before I saw Laban's grin.

"And what happens if I refuse to give you the Brass Plates?" he asked.

Nephi glanced at Sam, but Sam's face was frozen in fear.

"God will smite you!" Nephi threatened, but his voice was hollow. After all his talk about God making every-thing possible, he was still afraid of Laban. "And God will still give us the Plates of Brass."

Laban laughed, clapped his hands, and called his guards. Within moments, everything was taken off the floor and was out of our hands. The wagon was ordered seized and brought in.

We had lost everything.

"And now you have a choice, all of you. You can leave here or you can run from me like small children or you can stay and fight me like men." He drew a huge sword and brandished it. He had always been known as a good swordsman, even when he was drunk. He would make a contest of it. How many drinks he could swallow and still hold his sword properly.

"God will protect us. He will hold your sword in place. Or make it break," said Nephi. His eyes were wide.

What a kid! He would have made an interesting second in a duel of swords. Too bad we would never see that happen, since swords were not going to be going with us into the desert.

"We'll go," I said, holding up my hands. I wasn't going to go back to the wilderness and tell Father I'd lost all of our earthly possessions, plus my younger brother, and I still didn't have those stupid Brass Plates.

"You will be sorry for this!" said Nephi. "God will smite you!"

I grabbed his arm and flung him toward Lemuel. "Get him out of here!" I hissed. It was up to me to be the last man in the room with Laban. I blamed Nephi for the humiliation it cost me, though I should have blamed God instead.

I heard Lemuel stumbling backwards with a muttering Nephi, then heard him getting quieter, until there was nothing left to hear.

"Thank you," I said, bowing with my hands held together in prayer. "Thank you for letting us go. You are a generous and merciful man. An honorable man."

Laban nodded, a wide smile on his face. He was a little drunk, I thought, or he would not have been so magnanimous as to let us go.

"I always liked you, Laman. You are the clever one, despite what people say."

I did not ask him what people said.

"Without you those brothers of yours would be long dead, I think. They do not know how to hold their tongues."

"I am very sorry," I said. How much longer would I have to put up with this?

He raised his eyebrows and I saw a strange, calculating expression on his face. "You could stay here with me, Laman. Become one of my guards. I pay well. You can ask the others."

Was he serious? Stay here with him? He seemed just as likely to kill me as to pay me my weekly sum. On the other hand, did I really want to go back to the desert?

"You are very kind. But I have to look after my brothers," I said. "I'm sure you understand. You have brothers, don't you?"

"My brothers are dead," said Laban, and he swung the sword at me.

I realized only after it had gone over my head that he had never meant to kill me. Only to get a reaction.

He laughed.

I choked on the breath I'd thought I'd never take in again.

"Go on, then. You feel filial duty. That would make you useless as a guard in any case," said Laban, nodding at the door, his sword at his side.

I looked back. Was he really going to let me go this easily?

"Thank you again," I said, and bowed.

He turned away and I fled. I caught sight of Lemuel, Sam, and Nephi near the walls of the city and I chased after them.

12

It was a long time before we stopped running. But at some point, we saw a rock cave and the four of us ran into it and collapsed.

I was dripping sweat, cold and clammy as if I was ill, and my legs were shaking.

I thought of Father's face when we told him that we hadn't been able to get the Plates of Brass and we'd also given away everything in that wagon to Laban. Even though it had been Nephi's idea, and even though I'd done everything I could to make sure Nephi and Sam got out of Laban's house safely, Father would blame the failure on me and Lemuel. We should have thought of something better. We should have had our own vision, better than Nephi's.

I felt sick with guilt and a sense of smallness. I didn't want to prove Father wrong about surviving the wilderness anymore. I just wanted to survive and that seemed impossible.

We were all going to die if we didn't get back to Jerusalem. And we were going to die if we did go back to Jerusalem because now we'd made Laban angry enough that what remained of Father's wealth wouldn't be enough to protect us.

"I have to pray," said Nephi, turning his back to us. "I need to see a vision."

"Maybe you need to see your own backside," suggested Lemuel.

That got a weak laugh out of me.

Sam sniffed and I knew he was about to start crying, which I could not bear. He was too old to be a child and I was too young to pretend to be his father and comfort him.

"God has a plan for us. Even this is part of the plan. He is humbling us before He shows us that only He can grant us our desires," said Nephi, looking back at us briefly.

Humbling us? Or humbling me and Lemuel and Sam?

Before, Nephi had been so sure that God's plan was for us to give Laban everything we had so we could get the Brass Plates.

"My desires include wine, women, and some shelter from the sun," said Lemuel, his jaw very tight. He was about to explode with anger and Nephi didn't realize it. "Is God going to grant me those desires?"

Nephi ignored him. I don't think he even heard Lemuel speak. He was so miserable, I could almost feel sorry for him, despite all his arrogance.

"We should have hired another wagon," said Nephi. "We should have shown we were willing to give up even more."

"We brought everything we thought Laban would want. That wagon was piled high," said Sam in that almost-weeping tone. "And God didn't do anything to help us."

"I refuse to doubt God. We must get the Plates of Brass. I'll go back into the city and talk to Laban again," said Nephi. His jaw was as tight as Lemuel's was.

"Talk to him?" said Lemuel. "Oh, yeah. I'm almost tempted to go with you, just to watch that. He'll have you beaten to death before you get out a single word."

After having spent those last few minutes with Laban myself, I was pretty sure Lemuel was right on this point.

But Nephi raised his head and threw back his shoulders. "I'm not afraid to die for God's purposes to be achieved."

That was just too much for Lemuel. "And I am?" he asked. "You're saying I'm afraid?"

Nephi shrugged. "You want God to do everything for you. You want the Plates handed to you easily, without any risk," he said.

That was when Lemuel tackled him with an inchoate cry. Nephi tumbled down to the floor of the cave.

Before I could intervene, Nephi said, "You hate God, not me!"

Why couldn't he have said something kind and reconciliatory? Why couldn't he for one moment see someone else's perspective who didn't see following God as the only path?

"No, I hate you!" said Lemuel, kicking at Nephi's face.

Nephi didn't resist at all. He didn't huddle into a ball to protect himself. He didn't raise a hand to fight back. Did he want to be hurt? Did he think he deserved it and God was punishing him through Lemuel?

"Lemuel, stop it!" Sam tried to shout. He tried to get between Nephi and Lemuel and pull Lemuel back.

That was when I saw the staff on the floor of the cave. I didn't know how it had gotten there, but I grabbed it. For a moment, I hesitated because Lemuel was the one who had started this fight. I'd tried to protect Nephi so many times and he hadn't even noticed what I was doing. If I hit

Lemuel, he'd back off and be angry at me, but I wouldn't be physically harmed.

On the other hand, maybe it was time to teach Nephi a lesson. So far, he didn't seem to have learned anything about the real world.

So I started beating Nephi with the staff.

"You took everything from us!" I shouted. I aimed for the soft spots that everyone has, even someone as strong as Nephi: kidney, neck, and genitals. I wanted him to learn fast, for the sake of all of us.

He still didn't fight back, just opened his mouth in a silent howl and looked up at the roof of the cave as if staring at the heavens.

"Let me have that," said Lemuel, scooting away from Nephi and reaching for the staff.

"Stop it!" said Sam, also trying to take the staff from me. "Can't you see how hurt Nephi is? Just give him some time to rest. Then we can go back to Father."

"I'm not going back to Father without the Brass Plates. I will not fail him. God will find a way!" said Nephi again. He tried to stand up and fell back down.

I should have said that he'd had plenty and backed away from him. I should have shown some self-control. But I raised the staff again and brought it down on Nephi's head. It felt good to me. I admit it. I was that angry with him.

Then Lemuel found a rock and started hitting Sam with it.

"It's not my fault," he wept. And it was true. It wasn't.

Really, all of this was Nephi's fault. If he had just told Father no from the beginning, and had insisted that we all go back to Jerusalem, we would have all of our things.

I hit Nephi again, this time on his shoulders.

"Laman, you must pray to God," Nephi said in between blows. "He will tell you I am right."

If he had begged me for his life, I would have stopped. If he had howled in pain and shown he was human, I would have stopped. But he didn't. And I found myself beating him harder and harder. Blood splattered me when I got his eye. I saw him down on his hands and knees and that just made me angrier. I targeted his knees and ankles.

When he fell forward on his face, I leaped on top of him and would have finished him off if not for the bright light that suddenly made it impossible for me to see anything in the previously dark cave. I staggered back, unbalanced.

"Lemuel?" I said in a heavy voice. But my ears seemed to be filled with noise, a rushing sound that made no sense since we were not near a river.

"Why do you smite your younger brother with a rod?" said a voice unlike any I had ever heard before. It was soft and quiet, but it penetrated me to my core, made my heart shrink in my chest, and made me sweat like the noonday sun.

"He—he—" I stuttered, but I couldn't think of what else to say.

"Do you not know that God has chosen your brother to be a ruler over you?" said the same voice.

My eyes began to clear and I saw a hint of an outline. It was only a man, no larger than I was, but he was pulsing with energy and bright, white light. His eyes streamed with it. I didn't know what it was.

"God demands an answer. Do you understand that your brother has been chosen to be a ruler over you?"

I chittered something to agree. I think I would have agreed to anything at the moment.

"Your younger brother has faith to move mountains. He has the humility of a child. And he has done nothing to anger you save show himself better than you are," the man said.

I was trembling so hard I thought I would fall to pieces. But then the man put out a hand and touched me once.

All my fear was gone then. I knew that this man had been sent from God, for no one else had the power to make me feel so calm and peaceful.

"You will return to the city of Jerusalem and get the Plates of Brass from the evil man Laban. God does not intend to let the city remain for long where it stands, and before it falls, the Plates of Brass must be in the hands of those who will treasure them for the precious records which they are."

I murmured something in agreement. Whatever this man—or whatever he was—said, I would agree with it.

Then the man disappeared and I fell to the ground. It wasn't until late afternoon when I woke again to find that Lemuel was at my side that I realized he, too, had been affected by the light and the voice.

Sam and Nephi were standing over our heads, offering us skins of water which they must have found a place to fill somewhere.

"Who was that?" I asked quietly. Was he some friend of Nephi we didn't know about?

"An angel of God," said Nephi. And he did not speak again of the matter.

I knew that God had chosen my younger brother over me. I knew why. I didn't have to look far to feel my own weaknesses. I wasn't worthy to be the eldest son, the one Father entrusted the care of all his family to. No wonder

Nephi had been put in charge of this mission. No wonder I had been made to be a servant to him.

13

We slept in the cave that night, and woke early.

"I'm going back into the city," Nephi announced, looking out at the sun and sand.

"What? Why?" asked Lemuel, his voice thick with sleep.

I groaned and tried to stretch. Where were we? What was going on?

"How can you forget the angel who came to us last night? He said that I must return to Jerusalem and get the Plates of Brass from Laban. That is the will and commandment of God, and I will not ignore it," said Nephi.

"What are you going to do? Beg him for the Plates? It's not going to work," said Lemuel.

"God will tell me in the moment I need to know," Nephi said.

"Fine. Go. You can die all by yourself. We'll come and find your body in the street and take it back to Father," said Lemuel, putting his head back on his arm to go back to sleep.

"If I die, I die in God," said Nephi, voice strong and powerful as a prophet's. "But God sent an angel to protect me from death last night, so I believe He has plans for me yet. And if He must, God will send an angel to Laban, as well." He took a long drink from his water skin, and then stepped out of the cave.

"I'll go with you," I said, before I knew that I was going to make the offer. The angel had affected me, after all.

"No," said Nephi, holding up a hand and flexing his big muscles. "I don't want your help. Not anymore. Your lack of faith has clouded my mind already. I will go alone."

"But what about—" Sam began.

Nephi shook his head. "Not you, either, Sam." He thumped Sam on the back, then tried to do the same to Lemuel, who pulled back.

We watched him walk away from us, and then followed him from a distance. I'm sure he noticed us, but we stopped at the wall to the city, and found a spot where the heat wasn't terrible and we weren't likely to be seen by thieves or murdering bands that sometimes lurk outside the city for those who are unwary travelers. The last I saw of Nephi was of him holding out his hands to the guards at the gate to prove that he had no weapons.

In an hour, darkness fell and it began to grow very cold, waiting there outside the gates with nothing to keep us warm. We were too afraid to build a fire, and I could soon hear Sam's teeth chattering together. Lemuel swore now and again, as though the hot words would turn to fire.

I tried to sleep, tucking myself into the wall and curling into a ball. I dreamed that I stood over Laban and cut off his head. It was for Nephi's sake. I was taking vengeance, and I had waited until he was drunk and alone. Then I used his own sword and sliced his head quickly, without hesitation.

But once the head was off, I didn't know what to do.

"Laman?" I heard a voice calling me and woke from a stone cold sleep, jerking upright while my frozen hands clutched at my stomach.

"Laman, I'm here!" I heard again.

It was Laban's voice. He was here, taunting me. He had killed the defenseless Nephi and had come to tell me that we would never get the Brass Plates from him.

"Lemuel! Sam!" I called. "Beware!"

Then I threw myself at Laban with my knife. I wasn't sure I could get a good cut in before he strangled me, but I wanted to fight at close range. I wanted to see his eyes and feel his breath on me before I died.

"Stop it! It's me. Laman, it's Nephi," said the man I was tumbling with.

It wasn't until Sam called out, repeating what the man said that I stopped trying to attack him and realized that he wasn't trying to attack me in return. His hands were up in defense.

He looked exactly like Laban. He wore the same cloak, the same breastplate underneath. He wore the same sandals. He was the same size.

But he smelled of blood and death. I could see streaks of it on his scruffy beard, his hands, and his arms. And I thought of my dream. Maybe it hadn't been just a dream, after all. Maybe it had been a vision sent from God at last to me, though I was as unworthy now as I had ever been.

"Nephi?" I asked hoarsely.

"I have the Plates of Brass!" he announced proudly and held them up. "And Zoram!" he shouted and clapped his hands.

A man appeared from some distance behind Nephi. I knew him very well. He was the right hand man of Laban. Why was he here? If this was truly Nephi, what was going on?

Zoram stared at us. "What is this? What trap have you brought me into?" He turned to Nephi and held out an accusing finger. "You are wearing my master's clothes!

What have you done to him?" He put a hand to his lips, then called out, "Guards!"

Nephi looked terrified, but it was Lemuel and Sam who worked together to tackle Zoram. They held him down and stuffed one of Sam's shoes in his mouth so that he could not shout out anymore.

"I brought him with us. I figured that he might be useful in the end. And, well, I think that God wants him to come with us to the wilderness."

"Because there aren't enough of us who are going to die from lack of food and heat exhaustion," I said sarcastically, the words slow and tired as I was.

"God will protect us," said Nephi triumphantly. "And He will protect you, too, Zoram, if you come with us. You've already seen how God helped me to kill Laban when he would not give up the plates." Nephi looked deeply into Zoram's eyes, as he lay trapped on the ground.

Zoram resisted another moment, then went lax. "All right," he said.

"You promise to follow my father as a prophet of God?" Nephi asked.

"I promise," said Zoram dully.

He probably would have promised anything if it meant being set free. I stared at him, expecting him to bolt the moment he could. But he seemed almost mesmerized by Nephi, even now that he knew that he wasn't Laban. He knelt before Nephi as if before an idol. "Please forgive me," he said.

"You are forgiven," said Nephi and touched Zoram's shoulder and helped lift him to his feet.

From that time on, Zoram was a faithful servant and friend to Nephi. It wasn't fair, and I was filled with jealousy. I'd never had any friend other than Lemuel, not really. I'd never trusted anyone and they'd never trusted me. But here Nephi had killed a man and now his servant had changed loyalties in a matter of hours. Was this man crazy, too?

"Can we go home now?" asked Lemuel petulantly.

"We can go back to Father in the wilderness," said Nephi. "God fulfills His promises. He said that if we trusted in Him, He would make Laban give us the Plates. And so he did."

But Laban hadn't given them to Nephi, had he? At least not if the dream I'd seen was correct. My little brother, the one I'd always thought of as innocent and incapable of violence, even when pushed too far, had killed a man. Had God really told him to do that? Why would God want him to have blood on his hands like that?

It didn't make sense to me. I had always believed that I wasn't pure enough for God to have anything to do with me. Was Nephi going to face consequences from this? Would God stop speaking to him and turn to Sam instead? It seemed unfair to me, if this was the only way to get the Brass Plates. Why would God insist Nephi go back if He had known this would be the result? Did he hate Nephi, too?

Sam and Nephi were shaking their fists and shouting in jubilation. It didn't seem like either of them felt guilt or remorse now. Maybe Nephi never would. Maybe he was different from the rest of us.

But then I looked at Nephi closely and saw the blood-shot eyes and the small tremors in his hands. "What happened with Laban?" I asked. Did he need to talk about it? That could get it out of his system, at least the worst part, if he shared it with us. In a way, I suppose we were as guilty as he was.

"The Lord commanded me to slay him, in order to get the Plates. It is better for one man to perish than for a whole nation to dwindle in unbelief," said Nephi. He sounded as if he was repeating someone else's words without thinking about them.

14

We headed back to the cave and stayed there overnight. Zoram was still with us in the morning and he hadn't killed anyone, though I don't know why I was afraid of that anymore. Nephi had a power over him that I'd never seen even Father exercise.

Over the next several days, we made our way back to Father's camp in the desert.

As soon as we came close to it, I knew immediately that things had changed pretty drastically. For one thing, Father was sitting outside the tent and he looked like he hadn't eaten the whole time we were gone. For another thing, Father's clothes were filthy and his hair and beard didn't look like they had been combed for days. He looked like a beggar, and the whole camp was quiet as death.

As soon as Nephi and Sam saw Father outside the tent, they shouted to him, "Father!"

His head jerked to the side, but he didn't look toward them. He was staring off into the wilderness, and I could see that his eyes were wet and red, as if he were crying all the time.

Then Nephi called out again, "Father, we have them! We have the Plates of Brass!" He held them up over his head. He put them down next to Father, then embraced Father heartily.

"Nephi, my son! You're alive! You are all alive!" Father wasn't even looking at the unwrapped bundle of the Plates. He embraced Nephi first, and then Sam.

Finally, Father turned to me and Lemuel. "Thank you, Laman and Lemuel, my eldest sons, for doing as I asked of you. Thank you for watching over your younger brothers."

But I'd let Nephi go off and face Laban alone. I'd let my younger brother become a murderer because I was afraid.

"Now your mother will want to hear the good news!" Father turned to the tent and shouted for Mother. I wasn't sure why she hadn't heard him before, but when he came back out, his face was covered in some kind of liquid that looked and smelled—unpleasant.

Nephi might not notice it, but I did. Something had happened between Mother and Father while we were gone, something not at all good.

Mother came out of the tent, her hands held high and her face ravaged by fear. She looked as if she had aged ten years in the time since we had seen her last. Her beautiful skin was carved with wrinkles and her hair seemed to have fallen all out. She was as thin as Father had become, and she looked like she had lost everything in the world.

When she hugged Sam and Nephi, it was as if she was afraid to hold them too tightly, for fear they would fly away like dust. Or like ghosts.

"Are you really here? Are you really safe again?"

"Mother, I got the Plates of Brass. God is pleased with us. Now we can move onto the next phase of our journey to the Promised Land."

"I don't care about the Promised Land. I don't care anymore about your father's foolish dreams. I told him that if you returned, I would demand that you take me back to Jerusalem. If the city falls, the city falls, but at least I will have my sons around me. I will die with my family and not alone in the wilderness." She glanced at Father, and he cringed.

Sometimes I thought that Father had too much power over her. It was good to see that for once, she had stood up to him and demanded that she wasn't going to just meekly follow him. She had pushed him out of the tent for probably the whole time that we were gone. And she wasn't just going to forgive him because we had come back safe, after all.

"Mother, we can't go back now." There was a bit of a pause.

I waited to hear if Nephi would admit to anyone that he had given all of our worldly possessions to Laban, and for nothing. That wasn't how he had gotten the Brass Plates. But Nephi didn't tell her.

Instead, he said, "God has blessed our family greatly. He will provide for us as we continue into the wilderness. He will bless us. We will have better lives in the Promised Land than we could ever have imagined in Jerusalem. One day we will look back on all of our trials and laugh at them. We will rejoice in the life that God has given us," said Nephi.

"I don't want one day," said Mother mulishly. "I want this day. I want happiness now. I want a little ease in my older years. I want servants and a house over my head and food brought to me to eat."

Mother had spent so long without any of that, and she had only had a few years to enjoy it all. My poor mother.

"Nephi brought us a servant into the wilderness," I said, gesturing at Zoram, whom no one had introduced or asked about.

"A servant?" said Mother.

"Yes, God sent him to us," said Nephi, as soon as he realized how he could use this.

"He is not my servant. He is not a woman who can help me with what I need help with," said Mother. "Laman, you will come home with me, won't you?"

Nephi looked at me with pleading in his eyes. If Mother went home, she'd find out what he had done with all of her wealth.

"No, Mother," I said. I guess the angel had changed me, after all. The truth was, I didn't want to turn my back on God and join in the evil of the city of Jerusalem. "I want to find the Promised Land. I wanted to do one thing right in my life."

If Father had been there, maybe he would have praised me. But I seemed to have a knack for saying the wrong thing at the wrong time to the wrong person. She wasn't pleased with me.

"What? Laman, you can't mean that. You can't want to live in tents, in the sand. You can't want to be dirty every day, and to eat insects and raw flesh of animals. You can't want to wander through a wilderness, never knowing if you will find water again," said Mother.

She was right. I didn't want any of that. But after what Nephi had done, killing a man alone, it seemed a small sacrifice to make in comparison. God had already found out that I could not be as valiant as Nephi was, but I could do this one small thing. I could follow. God needed prophets and leaders. But perhaps He needed me and Lemuel, as well. The weak-minded, the easily frightened, the doubting. We were His children, even if we didn't always want to be.

"Lemuel, say you'll go back with me!" Mother cried.

I tensed, sure that Lemuel would be happy to go with her. Even if they didn't have what we'd put in the wagon, there were other things left. The house. And Lemuel could get work and earn money. He could do what he wanted. I didn't know what that was right now. I'd stopped talking to my dearest friend, my brother Lemuel. How had that happened? It was because of Nephi, and because of the angel.

To my relief, Lemuel said only, "I'd rather stay with Laman," and turned away from Mother.

"Then I will go without any of you!" said Mother. And she began to walk forward, hunched over, through the sands. I watched her stumble twice in a few minutes, then turned away.

Sam called after her, "Mother, stay. Mother, you can't go alone. It's too dangerous!"

I did not think Mother would survive the journey back alone. She did not have a good sense of direction and she was not sturdy. She had already suffered in the wilderness. But we'd have to wait until she was very weakened before we could force her back.

"Father, go after her!" I shouted.

He shook his head sadly. "She must make her own choice. No one is forced to go to the Promised Land. God only offers His blessings to those who ask for them. There is always a choice."

"She is your wife! She is the mother of your children. You can't let her die in the desert."

"I can't make her stay with me if she chooses to go," Father said in return.

It was ridiculous. Why should a son, even an eldest one, have to save his own parents' marriage? But I did it. I chased after Mother, convinced I could talk her into coming back before she was close to death.

She did not appreciate my gesture. She pushed at me several times and tried to trip me. Then she turned and said, "Go away, Laman. Let me die in the desert. Clearly, I am not worthy of this Promised Land of your father's."

I felt a well of sympathy in my heart. I knew what it was like to feel unworthy. And I wasn't going to let her be alone.

I stopped trying to argue with her and just kept walking at her side. Hours later, when she collapsed, I held her in my arms and offered her the last few swallows of water I had left in my skin.

"Are you ready to return to Father?" I asked her.

She held her lips tightly together. It was several minutes still before she gave in. My mother was a stubborn woman. And if she was not strong physically, she was strong in other ways. I will always remember that about her. It was the same strength now that had helped us all to survive when Father was gone. It made me think about what kind of a woman I wanted in my own life. An obedient one? Or a self-sufficient one?

"I love him, you know, Laman," she said at last, her voice shaking as she spoke. Her skin, as I held her, was hot and dry to the touch. I wanted nothing more than to get her back to some water, and to the shade and protection of the tents in the valley by the river. But I let her speak, because she needed to speak. And to be heard.

She went on: "Do not doubt my love for your father. I love him more than life itself. I have always loved him. It is why I have remained at his side, through all of our trials."

She had received more than one offer of marriage during the years when Father was gone. She could have pretended that Father was dead, or that he had left her. She could have divorced him. But she never did.

"But he expects too much of me. He takes my sons away and wants me to rejoice. He does not see my pain. He is always caught up in that visionary world of his. It is as if he has forgotten what the rest of us live like because he spends too much time communing with God."

She was jealous of his time with God. I could understand that very well. I was jealous, too.

I held her for another hour, feeling her breath move in and out of her body, praying to the God who had so rarely listened to me before that he would lend strength and life to her. This is the only thing I will ever ask, I swore to him. I will follow Nephi from now on. I will go to your Promised Land and do whatever you want me to do there. So long as my mother is there with us all, living and well.

I thought she was dying in my arms. I thought I would have to bury her here or take her body back to the camp, to Father, and help him bury her there. But I felt something change. I felt her take a sharp breath, and then she tensed all over, as if something was surging through her. After that, she opened her eyes and breathed steadily again.

"I am ready to go back now," said Mother a few minutes later.

I carried her back, my body aching with the pain. At last, I set her down in the tent she shared with Father. Father was waiting for her there.

"I knew you would come back. God sent me a vision," he said.

I think that was what made her cry at last. She threw her arms around him, wetting him with her tears, and sent me away.

"Well done, Brother," said Nephi to me, as I turned away from the tent.

"I didn't do it for you," I said. He hadn't helped me with her when she ran away. Did he love her at all?

"Well, then, God is pleased with you as well," he added.

Was He? I felt invisible ropes around me, tying me to my younger brother. My mother was alive. She might have died without God's blessing. And I would do what I must do to repay my debt. But that did not mean I would like it.

Lemuel and I went back to the tent and we slept inside those tight quarters with Nephi and Sam, who must have been having dreams like Father's. I did not have any dreams. I slept and I woke and thought of how much my mother loved my father and wondered if I would ever find a woman to love me like that.

But I knew it was impossible. A woman out here in the wilderness would be rightly miserable. I would be forever apologizing for her. We would have to wait to find women in this Promised Land God had in store for us. We'd just have to live with the loneliness along the way.

I had been lonely before. I knew it well. I had survived it then and I would survive it again.

15

Nephi announced the next day that he had dreamed a dream of a beautiful woman who was meant to be his wife. She was pure and she loved God and he knew that God was telling him that she must come to the Promised Land with him.

"God does not want us to be lonely in the wilderness," he declared to Father.

He didn't?

"I have had no dream," said Father. "Why would God not send such a dream to me?"

We were eating a breakfast that Lemuel and Sam had worked on together. It was barely edible. They had both caught birds and tried to roast them, but they hadn't done a good job of taking the feathers off. I was pulling out feathers all morning, pretending that I was using them to clean my teeth.

Nephi hadn't eaten anything. He said that he was fasting for God's will to be shown to Father, to send us back to Jerusalem again. "The woman I saw in the dream is the daughter of Ishmael, our cousin."

I remembered Ishmael well enough. He was younger than Father and he had given Mother money on several occasions when Father was away in the early years. When Father came back, Ishmael had been one of the few people who had invited us to eat with him, even after Father began preaching repentance in the city and became rather unpopular.

Ishmael had even found Mother one night on the streets, covered with filth that had been thrown at her by those who saw her near Father during one of his least popular speeches. Father didn't think about the backlash on Mother.

After that, Mother never went out of the house herself. She always sent servants for her instead. She pretended that she didn't care, that she liked staying at home and resting her "old bones," as she called her body. But I saw the fear in her eyes when she didn't want anyone to see, especially not Father. She had to protect him even still.

She loved him deeply, and even if I thought she was wrong, I was envious of that unconditional love Father had. Nephi getting it before I did was just too much for me to bear. I'd protected him as well as I could, but I wasn't going to celebrate him finding a wife if I had to live a solitary life until we got wherever the Promised Land was supposed to be.

"What about Lemuel and me?" I asked Nephi. "Do we get to go back to Jerusalem and find brides, too?" Was it possible that God had heard me last night, though I had not prayed directly to Him? I couldn't imagine a woman who would choose to live like this, but if Nephi could find one, why couldn't I? I wouldn't be picky. I might even consider that sometimes God heard my prayers, too.

"I will pray about it," said Nephi. And he went immediately away from us, so that he could pray in private. In an hour, he came back. "God has told me that we are all to marry the daughters of Ishmael. He has many daughters, and they are all of marriageable age."

And if they were the right age, then of course they would marry us, right? Why didn't Nephi consider the possibility that none of Ishmael's daughters would want us or the lives we would be offering them? They would be moving from the comfortable home of their father and into—well, tents. In the desert. In the middle of nowhere. Far from Jerusalem.

I guess the only hope we had was that Nephi could convince them that Father had been right about Jerusalem's imminent destruction. But there had been no sign of it when we were there last, and Father's calls to repentance had been universally ignored. Even Ishmael had pitied Mother. Why would he allow his daughters to be placed in an even worse situation?

I didn't believe it, but I suppose I was desperate enough to hope it was true. Even if I didn't get to pick my own wife, which was something I would have expected as the least of my rights as the son of a wealthy man in Jerusalem, if Nephi could convince Father to let him do this, I was going to be on his side.

What I thought was interesting was that Nephi was so insistent that this dream was from God. It was so obviously what Nephi wanted for himself. He was always pretending to be above carnal thoughts and fleshly desires—like the ones that plagued me and Lemuel. But clearly, he wasn't.

"Do you think that Ishmael will come willingly? Or do I need to come with you?" Father asked Nephi.

I sighed a little at the thought of what was sure to be the first in a long list of times when Father asked Nephi for advice, instead of the other way around. Wasn't Father supposed to be the visionary man? Wasn't he the one with the dream of Jerusalem's destruction that had sent us away from the city? Wasn't he the one who knew where the Promised Land was supposed to be?

"No!" said Mother sharply. "You will not go to Jerusalem with Nephi. You will not leave me here alone in the wilderness."

Father turned back to her as if he had—just for a moment—forgotten that she existed.

"Of course not. I will stay with you, then," said Father humbly.

"I'll go with Nephi!" Sam volunteered.

Lemuel looked at me, and I nodded. I was utterly selfish in this. I wanted a chance to make sure this would go well for me. If I let my brothers go without me, they'd pick out the best of Ishmael's daughters for themselves and I would be left with the ugly one.

"We'll go, too, Nephi," said Lemuel.

Nephi looked us over as if trying to decide if he wanted us to come with him. But how could he argue when it was his own prayer to God that had said we were to all have wives?

Father seemed pleased that we were in accord, even if we weren't. "Thank you! Thank you, Laman and Lemuel. I know I can trust you to watch over my younger sons yet again," he said.

This made me feel a twinge of guilt, since I hadn't done much to protect Nephi before. He'd kept going off on his own. If I could have, I would have slain Laban for him, but he never gave me a chance. God didn't, either.

We packed up a few things again and headed out. By now, I think we all knew the path to the city well enough not to worry about getting lost.

Nephi talked incessantly about his glorious vision of Ishmael's daughter intended for him from God. I wanted to hit him, because even when we stopped to sleep, he'd murmur in his sleep about her. The rest of us just wanted a chance to think about our own hopes.

For the first time in a long time, I wished that I looked better. I wanted to go back to the house and find some nice clothes, clean up, and cut my hair and beard. I wanted to put on some cologne so that I didn't smell of the desert, and I tried to think of what I would say to a woman who I might live with for the rest of my life.

Should I try to flatter her? Woo her? Tease her? Should I try to show her my real self or hide it from her? I felt as unsure of myself as I'd been when I was Nephi's age, and I wished that I could feel as confident as he did that God would make us all happy. Why would God want to make me happy? What had I ever done for God?

When we reached Jerusalem for the second time, we got past the gates easily enough and then I let Nephi lead us to Ishmael's home, though I could perfectly well have done it myself. Sometimes Nephi acted like Lemuel and I were idiots, but what did I care?

I worried about Laban's family searching for Nephi. They must have found his body by now, and realized that the Plates of Brass had been taken by someone who was close to him in size—like Nephi. The fact that Nephi had been to Laban's twice before demanding the Plates would make it easier to suspect him.

Yet Nephi did not seem to think of any of that at all. He was completely focused on Ishmael and God's promise that we would marry his daughters.

When we arrived at his home, Ishmael welcomed us in eagerly. He insisted on feeding us before we spoke of our reason to visit. I think he believed that Father had gone mad, and that we had just escaped him and were looking for refuge. His daughters served us, and then stayed to watch us and listen to us talking to him and his two sons.

Three of the daughters were exactly as beautiful as Nephi had said they would be: skin without a blemish, lips red as rubies, breasts full, hips swinging with the intention to attract attention. The fourth one was larger than the others, thick lips, and a nose that had been broken and healed crooked. Her feet were large and she wore no slippers. Her dress was made of black fabric that shimmered but seemed like the sky in a sandstorm. She had a clouded expression on her face and every movement seemed angry.

Her name was Naomi and I was terrified of her, though she did not pay any attention to me. There was something about her that made me sure that she would change my life and when Lemuel whispered to me about her being the ugly one and that we should try to make sure she chose Nephi, I looked away and refused to answer. I could not imagine Nephi marrying her. She would hate that he was more handsome than she was, and I could not imagine her simply agreeing to everything Nephi said. She did not deserve him.

I had missed part of the conversation between Nephi and Ishmael, but Ishmael nodded thoughtfully and told Nephi that he would pray overnight about joining us. Ishmael's three daughters giggled and waved to us, then disappeared. The fourth, Naomi, was the last to leave and she stared at me long and hard, as if she were trying to memorize the face of a man she intended to take her revenge on.

What had I done to her? Nothing, but I wanted to apologize to her nonetheless. I didn't know what had broken her nose, but I could only think that I knew what it was like to be the one who wasn't favored by God, surrounded by those who were.

16

I dreamed about Naomi that night. I thought I saw her as a young girl, when she was as beautiful as the others. I saw a man who claimed to love her beat her mercilessly when she had refused him a kiss. She was bleeding on the ground and I could see her face change from hurt to angry. That was the face I knew. She had been wounded by the one she had expected to love and protect her. I knew what that was like, too.

I woke up longing for her and thinking that I would fight any of my brothers to the death if they thought they could take Naomi from me. I had only known her for a few hours and I already felt like this for her. I hadn't even spoken to her privately. What was wrong with me? I had no reason to believe that she would feel anything for me at all. After that beating, maybe she could never love a man again. But I couldn't help hoping that she might see something in me, as well.

Ishmael looked very grave when he returned to us in the morning, and I was sick with fear that he would tell us to leave and go back to the desert without him or his daughters.

But it was his children and his wife he delivered the bad news to. He commanded them to pack up as much as they could carry and told them that they were leaving Jerusalem to go to the Promised Land with Lehi and his family. He said that God had spoken to him as clearly as if

He had been standing in the room, and that he could not turn his back to God's commands.

His wife began to weep loudly, and all of the daughters but Naomi did, as well. The sons were stoic about it. I thought I could see Lemuel making eyes at one of the other three daughters, but Nephi seemed too proud to do the same and Sam seemed too awkward. Every time he looked at the girls, he reddened and started to choke. He was too young to marry anyway, I thought.

Nephi volunteered us to help pack and carry. Ishmael's family had plenty of tents, blankets, and water skins, and food, dried and fresh. But when the daughters brought their packs out, we all stared at how much they expected us to carry for them. Naomi was the only one who was willing to shoulder some of the family items in addition to her own. I watched her bend over and then begin to walk as her father chastised the other girls and told them they could not take more than they could carry for themselves.

She might not be as lithe and beautiful as her sisters, but I could not look away from her. Her muscles rippled underneath her dark dress. She was the kind of woman who could survive in the wilderness, I thought. She wouldn't complain about having to kill her own prey or about plucking feathers from birds before they were roasted. She would be a worthy companion and a mother of strong children.

I felt a moment's anxiety that Nephi might take her from me, but then I saw Nephi comforting one of the other girls and relief flooded me. That didn't mean that Naomi would take me as a husband, but at least I would have a chance to woo her—if I could figure out how.

The first night we camped, I went to hunt. I didn't have the bow and arrows we'd left with Father, but I set a trap I built with my own hands. I caught a bird in it after only a few hours and brought it to the girls' tent that Naomi was sharing with her sisters. There was no way to knock on the tent door, so I cleared my throat a few times until one of the other sisters, Rachel, I think her name was, opened the flap and looked at me.

"Naomi, the ugly old one is here for you."

Did they all know that I had my eye on Naomi? I flushed, and tried not to show any embarrassment as Naomi came out into the dying light, squinting at me. "What is it?" she asked.

I held up the bird and showed it to her.

She said nothing, made no movement.

"It's a bird," I explained, thinking maybe she'd been so privileged she didn't know what meat looked like before it was cooked. "For dinner."

"We've already eaten," she said.

There was laughter from her sisters in the background. She could have stepped outside with me, so that we were away from them, but she didn't.

"Oh, but I thought this would taste better," I said. I assumed that all they'd had for dinner was some fruit and some dried meat. No one had built a fire that I had seen.

She yawned loudly. "I'd like to go to bed now. I've had a very long, hard day and tomorrow doesn't look to be any better."

Was it my fault she was here in the wilderness? I suppose it was, in some sense. If Nephi had gone back only for one of the daughters, rather than all of them, she might have stayed in Jerusalem with her mother. Was that what she wished had happened? Of course it was. What a dolt I was being. Any sane person would prefer to stay in a glorious city like Jerusalem rather than live here in the sand.

"If you pluck off the feathers and gut it, it will make a good meal in the morning," I suggested, still holding the bird out to her, though not as happily. I had the sense now that I smelled badly and that the bird wasn't any better.

"Pluck the feathers and gut it?" repeated Naomi dully. She shook her head. "I don't cook. My sisters cook. Perhaps you'd like to give it to one of them."

There was more laughter in the tent behind us.

I think I have never felt more humiliated in my life. And yet, I stood there and took it. I would take whatever she offered, so long as she would keep looking at me.

"Or you could take it into your tent and cook it yourself," Naomi suggested.

I already knew that I wasn't very good at that, and I'd never felt less hungry in my life.

I wished that I hadn't gone hunting. I should have stayed in the camp and talked to her. I could have shared whatever she had for dinner. I could have done a thousand other things than the one I had chosen.

"I should have done something else," I said in a low murmur. Would she give me any hint about what it might be that would make her happy?

"Yes, you should have," she said. But she offered no suggestions.

Then one of the sisters, Esther, I think it was, came up and took the bird from me. "Naomi doesn't cook," she said. "If you want a wife with any of those skills, she's not the woman for you."

Naomi could have been embarrassed, but I saw no sign of it. She shrugged at me and then said, "They won't share any of it with you, you know," nodding back at her sisters.

All my work for nothing, and I didn't care. I still just wanted her to like me, just a little. "If you don't cook, what do you do?" I blurted out.

Her eyes brightened. "I like hunting," she said.

Well, that was unusual, but on the other hand, why shouldn't a woman hunt if she was as strong as Naomi clearly was? "Would you like to go hunting with me tomorrow night, after we've camped for the day?"

"We won't have arrived yet—at wherever it is we're going?" she asked.

I shook my head. "It's at least three days, probably four with your sisters and mother." As soon as I said it, I wished I hadn't. It sounded like I was criticizing the women for being slow, and I didn't mean it that way. It didn't matter to me how long it took us to reach the river in the valley where Father and Mother were. As far as I was concerned, we could spend another year traveling to our destination. As long as I was with Naomi.

"Well, then, I will go hunting with you," said Naomi.

"Not by yourself!" a voice called out from the tent.

I hadn't thought about that. It wouldn't be appropriate for us to be alone together hunting, of course. I was about to suggest that I'd take Lemuel and Sam with me, or her brothers if she preferred. But Rachel came over to us and said, "We'll go with you, Naomi."

"Hunting?" said Naomi, who seemed as dismayed by the idea as I was.

"Of course, hunting," said Rachel. "I can't imagine anything we would rather do." More laughter from the tent.

I looked at Naomi. I knew she didn't want her sisters to come with us, but what other choice did we have? I wanted to spend time with her, and this was the only way we could manage it. So hunting with sisters it would be.

I went to sleep that night and dreamed of killing a lion and showing Naomi the corpse, only to have her show me her kill—an even larger lion. I wasn't sure what the dream meant, but I didn't ask Nephi for his opinion. We packed up the next morning and traveled until it got too hot. We found some shelter and rested until it was cooler again. Then we traveled until it was night, under Nephi's orders.

How was I going to take Naomi hunting in the dark? In the desert? It seemed impossible. Nephi was deliberately making things difficult for me. I hadn't told him about my plans, but he must have heard about them. From the pointing and whispers all through the day, I thought everyone in the group must have heard about my interest in Naomi by now.

She ignored me completely, and I was sure that when I appeared at her tent, she'd tell me she wasn't interested in hunting anymore.

On the contrary, she had changed into trousers and tunic and had a bow and arrow herself that was just as well made as what we'd left with Father. She told me proudly that she had made it herself.

"She has skills, just not any of the ones a man is looking for," Rachel told me with a smirk as she tries to tie her skirts into trousers since she apparently did not have the same wardrobe flexibility as her sister.

The other two daughters of Ishmael covered their faces and hung back while Rachel and Naomi and I were a threesome. I forgot completely about hunting until Naomi reminded me once we were out of range of the noise of the camp.

"Stand back or she'll hunt you," Rachel said with a laugh as Naomi took out her bow and nocked it.

"Shhh!" Naomi hissed at us.

I couldn't see what she could, but I went very still and quiet.

Her arrow flew and I heard a brief sound of exhalation and then a thump to the sand.

Naomi ran forward to grab her prey and then brought it back to me. Not only had she bested me in accuracy and speed, she had killed a striped hyena large enough to feed the whole camp, not just season a pot of stew. She held it high and offered it to me.

I took it, not realizing that I was now giving up my position as hunter and becoming her assistant instead. She killed two more animals that night, two hares that were smaller than the hyena, but still better than a bird. We turned back after that, the sisters back to laughing in their own conversation while I was behind them, loaded down with the prey.

Once we were back in camp, Naomi showed what she was good at: lighting a fire. It was a bonfire and she had collected wood as we came back through the desert to feed it. I had not even noticed what she was doing, though she was carrying far more weight than I was.

We feasted that night. Naomi's sisters eagerly skinned and gutted the animals and put them on sticks to roast over the fire. I admit that the tastes I had were delicious, but the thought of giving up my place as hunter was not something I worried over. Naomi had bested me fairly and instead of being embarrassed about it, I found myself proud of her. This was a woman to rejoice over, to fight over, if necessary.

But when I watched carefully that night, I could see that no one saw her as I did. My brothers were all interested in the more typically beautiful sisters, not the glory that was Naomi. I only had to convince her that I was her equal.

We arrived back at the valley two days after the hunt and Father and Mother rejoiced to see us again, though they did not seem as surprised as they had before, when we came back with the Brass Plates. Father embraced Ishmael and welcomed his family officially into our camp, offering him the best place to set his tent, near the river.

After that, the pattern developed that would continue for some months. Naomi and her sisters would go out hunting while I went out with my brothers. We rarely came back with anything better than she did, even with Nephi's bow to help us. Lehi would read scriptures to us as the meat roasted and our mouths watered.

I tired of this after some time. I was only getting to see Naomi from afar, and though she had a wonderful figure to watch, I wanted more than that. So one morning, my frustration at its height, I worked my way through the crowd of people around Lehi's reading and reached Naomi at last. I touched her on the elbow to get her attention. She looked at me and I thought she understood what I meant. I motioned to the river and waited until Lehi was at a dramatic part of his scripture reading.

Then I pulled on Naomi's arm, and as she stumbled toward me, I held tightly to her and pushed her forward. I thought we were escaping the boring scripture study and could go off and enjoy some time in the river, or perhaps just walking together. No need for hunting or sisters or brothers to accompany us. My intentions were completely innocent, I assure you.

I don't know if I startled Naomi or if she did it to teach me a lesson, but instead of following along with me, she took one step forward, then pulled back on my arm, nearly yanking it out of the socket.

I let out a moan of pain that I tried to stifle, still thinking that I didn't want to draw attention to myself in case we could get away freely.

But when I still had not let go, Naomi's full fury was unleashed. She kicked at my knees and I went down hard on the sand. I didn't think to defend myself because this was Naomi, the woman I loved. I did not want to hurt her and still didn't understand why she was fighting against me.

"Naomi!" I cried out.

She kicked me between the legs then, which made me fall forward on my face into the sand. I whimpered and tried to hold myself. Surely I was no longer a threat to anyone at that point.

Nonetheless, Naomi climbed on top of me, put her arms around my neck and might have strangled me to death if Nephi hadn't come along and rescued me.

"Let him go. He'll be good now, won't he, Laman?" He lifted up my head enough that I could see Naomi.

She had her teeth bared like a warrior, but I think I saw some regret in her eyes. She had not intended to take it this far.

Then I remembered the dream I'd seen of her, with the man who had beaten her. She must have trained herself to react violently when she felt threatened. And I had surprised her. She had done this before she had even thought about it.

Nephi and Sam helped carry me back to my tent. They asked if I wanted Ishmael's wife, who was known as a healer, to come minister to me, but I told them I would be fine by morning. It was not a pleasant night. I did not sleep much, even when Lemuel came to bring me some wine he had taken from Ishmael's house when they were packing. He'd been saving it for himself, and it showed true brotherly devotion when he offered it to me.

"She isn't worth it," said Lemuel.

But she was worth it. I wanted Naomi and none other. Her sisters seemed like pale imitations to me.

"It was my fault," I said. I didn't explain about the dream because it was none of Lemuel's business and I was already beginning to feel protective toward Naomi. She didn't need my physical protection, but that didn't mean she couldn't be hurt.

Two days later, in the hot hours of the day, we were playing by the river when Naomi and her sisters came toward us. Naomi looked determined, like she was hunting again and this time she had human prey on her mind. I set my jaw and refused to show any fear. I wanted her to want me. Why should I turn away?

The sisters explained to my brothers about the rules of the game. We threw lots and they determined who was to kiss whom. The sisters laughed when Nephi flushed and said that this game was not of God. It was not sober or righteous. But Rachel, the one he liked, whispered to him after he left and brought him back.

The first lot thrown let Nephi kiss Rachel, which stopped his complaints about the game. Then Lemuel was to kiss Esther. There were two men and two women after that.

I tried not to look too pointedly at Naomi as I threw the next lot. I was so sure that it would have Naomi's name on it that I stared in horror when I saw Ruth instead. I looked up at her.

She was beautiful in every way that I once would have considered important for a wife. I did not mean to hurt her feelings, but I could not imagine kissing her with any real passion. I could see her look at Sam and it was obvious how she felt for him. I did not want to insult her, but nor did I want Sam to react badly to this foolish game.

In the end, it was Naomi who bellowed as she moved closer to me. "He's mine!" she declared to her sisters. She pushed Ruth out of the way, grabbed hold of me by my shirt and pressed her lips firmly to mine.

It was a kiss unlike anything I had dreamed about before. I felt breathless and overcome. I felt as if I was no longer in control of myself, as if I had been sucked into Naomi's body by the pressure of her lips. I was drowning and delirious with joy at the same time.

Naomi pulled back, looked at me. "You are mine," she said.

"Ummph," was all I got out before she kissed me again, harder than before.

And that, it seemed, was that.

17

Some weeks later, as we all became used to life in tents in the desert valley by the river, Naomi and I spoke often of marriage and our future together. We tried to imagine what it would be like when we were settled where we were going, but it was impossible since Nephi would never tell us anything about it except that it was "The Promised Land." North, south, east, west, in the mountains, in the desert, by the seashore, Nephi did not know.

"You haven't seen the vision that Nephi has of this Promised Land?" Naomi asked me as we sat in my own tent. We were betrothed now and were allowed to spend some time together alone, without being interrupted by sisters, brothers, or parents.

"No," I admitted. "I haven't."

"But you believe it's real? You believe that God has spoken to Nephi?" She pressed me. She smelled of blood, because she'd just gotten back from hunting. The smell of meat cooking was filling the camp, and it made me love her even more than she could do anything she chose to do.

"I believe that Nephi believes that God speaks to him." Naomi had seen how Nephi acted as the leader of all of us, but I didn't like to admit that I had accepted it.

"But why not to you? You're the oldest. You should be your father's heir. Nephi is so much younger," said Naomi.

Younger, but more easily moved by the Lord. I thought of the angel that had come to save Sam and Nephi from a beating. I thought of the sandstorm Lemuel and I had been saved from. I knew God was real. I knew that God loved Nephi best, just as Father did. And I knew that Nephi deserved it because he was more obedient.

"You're strong. Why wouldn't God choose you to lead?" asked Naomi.

She was the woman I loved. I didn't want to admit my weaknesses to her. "He has confused my father," I said. "My father is an aging man and Nephi works on him, whispers to him about Lemuel and me being unworthy."

We were unworthy, but I could not say this.

"If Nephi were gone, you think your father would see you truly?" asked Naomi.

I thought we were talking in hypotheticals, so I said, "Yes, of course. He would have to."

"Then you know what you must do," said Naomi. She'd had a few encounters with Nephi and she didn't like him. She had seen his arrogance and she felt his judgment that she was not a proper woman because she hunted.

I think he was jealous of her, and perhaps even jealous of me, that I had already become betrothed to one of Ishmael's daughters before him, when he was the one who had had the first dream about returning to Jerusalem to ask their family to join us.

"I know what I must do," I echoed, though I truly didn't.

"You have to do something about Nephi. Only then will your father listen to you and give you your proper due as the oldest son," she said.

It is not Naomi's fault that I chose to do what I did next. It was all my own pride. It was what the worst part of me had wanted to do for some time. I had wanted to get rid of Nephi since he was born and I could see how much my father loved him and his new chance for life through him. I'd just never let myself consider how easy it would be to do what I wanted to him. I'd seen what happened when we attacked Nephi with the staff in the cave. He didn't fight back. He didn't want to hurt his brothers, even if we wanted to hurt him.

I found Nephi was already awake and praying, though the rest of the camp was quiet. Lemuel had just woken up and I motioned to him.

"Where's Sam?" I whispered.

"Still sleeping, I think, along with everyone else," he said, and motioned to one of the tents.

"Good." I told him my plan. We would bind Nephi with rope and we would leave him in the desert. Then we would talk Father into going back to Jerusalem, for Mother's sake. If God wanted a prophet, he could call someone else.

I felt a hot thrill of pleasure at the idea of hurting Nephi the way I'd wanted to for so long. It was what I should have done. It was what I had the right to do, as the older brother. God would surely look on this with favor and reward me, once I had proven that I believed in myself and had taken the power that Nephi had usurped from me.

I got the rope that was in my pack, plenty to set up a tent—or to tie up a young man.

"I will lure him to us," I said, handing Lemuel the rope. "Then I will grab him from behind and hold him while you get the rope around his legs. It can't take long because he is stronger than I am. You have to have it done before he realizes what is happening."

Lemuel nodded. "We could try to get him drunk first. Then he might fight us less." Lemuel always had access to wine. I don't know how, after weeks in the desert, but he was able to find a bottle or a skin somehow, as if that was God's gift to him.

"When was the last time you saw Nephi drink anything alcoholic?" I said, shaking my head. "You know that he thinks it is wrong. He says it makes him weak."

We would have to do this the hard way.

"I could help," said Naomi, who had heard much of what we had planned. At first I thought she would volunteer to hold Nephi down physically. She was probably strong enough for that, but it would be embarrassing for me to need help from my betrothed to get my younger brother in line.

Instead, she offered, "I'll tell him that my sister Rachel is ill. He is in love with her, and he'll be so worried for her that he'll be distracted."

I nodded to her. "Good plan," I said.

At that, Naomi went to tell Nephi her story, and I could see him coming toward us, his face grave, his eyes distant as if he were in prayer already.

I stepped in front of him, and he stopped cold for a moment. Just long enough for Lemuel to come up behind. Nephi tried to move to the side to get around me, but by then, his legs were already tied. He fell to the ground, letting out one small cry of protest, but that was all. Lemuel and I might not be as strong as he was, but we were crafty.

We dragged Nephi away from the camp, away from the river, and up into the rocks. We beat him thoroughly and then left him there, tied up. I told myself that he wasn't going to die there. He'd have shelter from the sun this afternoon, and after we were gone, he'd come back to consciousness, be able to get out of the ropes, and make his way to the river for water. He could decide then if he wanted to stay out here in the wilderness alone or if he wanted to come back to Jerusalem with the rest of us. With Nephi gone, I was sure that Father and Mother would be easier to convince about the foolishness of thinking there was some Promised Land out there.

Lemuel and I concocted a story on the way back to the camp. We'd tell them that Nephi had simply disappeared. A wild animal must have taken him. Too bad we hadn't thought to get some of Nephi's clothes dipped in blood to find in his tent. That would have helped, but I didn't want to go back now. It would take too much time and it was already getting hot.

I figured that Mother would cry a bit, but I braced myself for that. She cried frequently and we could help her walk through the desert if necessary. We could carry her if we had to.

In the end, it was Rachel, Naomi's sister, who made everything impossible. She began weeping and wailing at the thought of Nephi's death. She insisted that we must make a monument of some sort to him. And then when she started looking for stones to mark this spot exactly, she heard him calling out for help.

I'd been so sure that we knocked him out long enough to get away, but as always, Nephi turned out to be stronger than we thought. He kept calling out and then Rachel went to get him. I could hear when she reached his position and he stopped shouting. I could just imagine what would happen when he came back and accused me of trying to murder him. No one would believe me then that I had only meant to shut him up for a while.

So I told the truth while I could. I explained to Ishmael, to his wife and his children, that they had to choose that very moment between returning to Jerusalem and to their easy lives there in luxury. Or they could stay here with Nephi and trust that at some point he really would get them to the Promised Land.

The choice was up to them for their family, but I said that Lemuel and I knew what we were choosing.

Ishmael and his sons hesitated. But Naomi and Esther, who was in love with Lemuel, came to stand by us. We were ready to start walking out toward Jerusalem, uncaring of who followed us and who didn't, when then I heard Nephi calling on the power of God in a loud voice to free him from the bonds his wicked brothers had put on him.

I knew in that moment that I was the wicked brother. Again. And God would listen to Nephi, because God always had. Just like Father. Nephi had been chosen from the moment he was born.

"You should have killed him," Naomi whispered to me.

I was surprised at her, but when Nephi came down to us from the rocks, I began to think she was right. What was it Nephi had said? Better for one man to die than for a whole nation to perish? Well, the nation of this family was going to perish in the wilderness if we kept following Nephi, I was sure. But no one was leaving now.

Nephi's voice was mesmerizing and as soon as he was in the camp, his figure was imposing. He had some kind of power that I would never be able to imitate. It was just within him, this faith in himself, this confidence that he was always right and if anything or anyone tried to stop him, God would be on his side and would save him.

I knew that we had lost, but I still argued as Nephi lectured us on why we could not return to Jerusalem, and why we should be grateful that God had chosen us, out of all the inhabitants of Jerusalem to save and to bring to the Promised Land.

"You are lucky that you have a prophet among you who could tell you God's plans for the future, and that you have God's blessings on you to protect you and keep you safe as we all journey through the trials of the wilderness and arrive at last at the Promised Land."

"He's the lucky one," Naomi murmured. "But that doesn't mean he will stay lucky."

18

In the morning, Father announced he had something "important" to tell his family. He woke us up by shouting outside of our tent. Lemuel and I grabbed a robe and hurried outside. I think some part of me was hoping that he'd have heard that we could go back to Jerusalem, after all. I should have known better.

"I have had a new vision from God," said Father. "I had to tell you all about it, for it pertains to your very lives, and your eternal salvations."

Oh, well, if it was about our eternal salvation, then by all means, wake us up when we could have been sleeping and preparing for another hellish day in the middle of the desert with only hunting to sustain us.

"I was wandering in a darkness when a man dressed in a white robe came to me. And then he was gone again."

When I had dreams like that, I usually assumed that they meant nothing more than that I'd eaten something bad the night before. I didn't think they were a vision from God. But Father was different. Everything was from God as far as he was concerned. And maybe it was. What did I know? Nothing but that God never spoke to me.

Father continued: "And then I saw an iron rod beside a raging river. There were many people holding to the rod, moving closer to a grand tree. I followed after them and when I reached the tree, I saw that it was full of the most delicious fruit."

Right when he got to that part, my stomach rumbled loudly. Lemuel broke out into loud laughter, but no one else laughed with us. When we were quiet again, Father began speaking as if we had never interrupted him.

"I partook of this precious fruit, white and delicious, fruit that was desirable above all other fruit, and then I turned around to see where my family was. I wanted to share of this fruit with all of you."

Good for you, Father. That makes you better than the rest of us. Because if I had found a thriving fruit tree in the middle of this desert, I would have eaten myself sick from it, or maybe shared a little with Naomi. I wouldn't have just taken one piece of fruit and then looked around to see who was watching me.

But Father was always a performer. He could never just enjoy something without people watching him enjoying it and seeing how lucky he was.

"I called out to Nephi and Sam, and to your mother. You made your way to the tree by holding to the rod and you partook of the fruit with me, and you were filled. I could see then that you turned back and tried to call to others. You wanted to share the fruit as I did."

Of course they did. They were the good sons. Lemuel and I were the ones who had supposedly just tried to kill Nephi.

I can't say I was surprised when Father said, "I saw that Laman and Lemuel were wandering by the river, and when I called to you, you did not heed me."

"We were probably thirsty," I said.

Lemuel grinned at me, but Father and the others were not amused. I had taken attention away from him and this was his story, not mine.

I noticed that Ishmael and his family had started to come out of their tents. Naomi looked over at me and I rolled my eyes at her. We both had problems with our fathers.

Father said, "I was worried for you, my older sons. I know that the fruit that I partook of represents the love of God. And because you did not partake of it, you would not be with us when we entered the happiness of God's eternal rest."

If God's eternal rest was anything like this desert, I think I could skip that part. As for the love of God, well, if our own Father didn't love us as much as Nephi and Sam, why should it be a surprise that his God felt the same way toward us? We were the wicked sons, the ones in the scriptures who always ended up dying one way or another because of their lack of piety.

"Laman, I am deeply worried about you and your brother," said Father, looking directly at me. "I feel that I have not done enough to teach you the scriptures and the ways of God. It is my fault that you are untrained, and now we have a chance for me to rectify those mistakes of my past."

I could feel everyone staring at us now.

"Before now, I allowed you to decide if you wanted to listen to the scriptures for yourselves. I thought that at some point, you'd hear the word of God and it would work on you to make you love the good. But that has not happened and now I have decided that you must sit and listen every day for the sake of everyone in this camp. You must learn to hear and rejoice in God's ways or all of us will be in peril.

His voice dropped and became more prophetic. "God has told me that we will not be able to move on to the

Promised Land from this place until we are all ready, just as the Israelites were not ready to enter the Promised Land until the old, unfaithful and wicked of the group had died and the younger rising generation had a chance to take control."

I was so tired of this manipulation. We had to earn Father's love? And God's? We didn't get to have the fruit of that tree until we listened to more scriptures? "We'll do better," I said, trying to bow my head and show more humility. "We'll pray with you. Every day. And listen to your scriptures."

"And we'll be obedient," Lemuel added. I was pretty sure he was thinking along the same lines as I was. We'd say whatever we had to right now, and then figure out how to get around what Father's plans for us were later.

"I am going to pray to God so that I can see my own vision of this tree," Nephi announced.

Of course he was. And God would probably give it to him.

"Laman and Lemuel, you should pray to God as well, and see if He will grant unto you the same vision. God gives to those who ask Him." Nephi was such an innocent at times. I suppose that was why God loved him so much. And why I hated him.

"God wouldn't tell us anything," said Lemuel. "Isn't that right, Laman?"

I felt a heaviness as I said the truth. "We're not like you and Father." We might see an angel once in our lives. We might feel God's presence here and there in a really rare moment. But we weren't in touch with Him permanently. We weren't crazy enough for that.

"God loves all His children," Nephi insisted. "Sam, you should pray, as well. God will give unto all who ask Him in faith. I believe in Father's dream, but I want to under-stand it, as well. What is the tree and what is the fruit? And what does the rod of iron mean? Why is there a build-ing with people mocking in it and why is the water that flows by dirty?"

Those were not the questions I would have asked about the dream. I would have asked why some people held onto the rod and some people wandered away. Why did some people care about the fruit and others didn't? I mean, if it was really the most delicious thing in the world, you'd think everyone would be mobbing the tree or planting new ones or something? Why would people hang out in a building far away from any food source?

My stomach growled. I guess I knew why my questions were about food. I was in a desert and I hadn't eaten any-thing but meat that Naomi had caught in days.

"What about Ishmael?" Sam asked. "And his daugh-ters? Why weren't they in the dream? Are they going to eat the fruit of the tree with us?"

"Ishmael must have his own vision. He must lead his family to the tree on his own. No one can do that for another man and his family," said Father.

I glanced at Naomi, but she shrugged. I think her father was beginning to doubt my father, but if so, he didn't say it right then. Ishmael had poked his head out of his tent and listened to the first part of what Lehi had to say, then gone back to sleep.

"Has he always been this crazy?" she asked me.

"Always," I said.

"But you follow him anyway?"

Did I? I was trying to follow God, but it was too hard sometimes. God asked us to do crazy things and Father and Nephi did them gladly. Then Lemuel and I got in trouble for being rational and asking questions about how this was really going to work.

"He's a prophet," I said. I still believed that, even if I didn't always do what my father said. God spoke to him and He didn't speak to me. The most I got were some dreams at night and an angel, no real voice telling me exactly what to do.

"He says he is. But anyone could say they're a prophet. You could say you're a prophet, too," Naomi pointed out.

I stared at her. Was she trying to tell me that's what she wanted me to do? To pretend to have a vision for my betrothed as Father had said that a man could have for his own family? What would I say I had seen? Would anyone believe that God had spoken to me? Would God strike me dead for blasphemy?

I shook my head at her. "Not now," I said.

"Then when?" she asked impatiently. "When will you become a man, Laman? I thought you were, but now I'm not so sure."

Was I a man or a boy? I'd never left my father's home and here I was in the wilderness with him, rebellious as any young teenager. She was right, and yet I still wasn't ready to turn my back on him. I'd tried it once and the sandstorm had brought me back here. Surely there had to be a reason for that. I just had to figure out what it was and stop doubting. I had to put aside my feelings for Nephi and listen to God through him.

Nephi disappeared into his tent to pray in private. Sam did the same thing, but he came out again in about an hour. Nephi was gone all day.

Naomi and I went out hunting and got two foxes to skin and roast for dinner, a good dinner. It was the only thing I seemed to be good at, and Naomi was better at it than I was. I couldn't do the spiritual work for our group. I could only do the dirty work, the physical labor. No wonder Nephi thought he was above me.

But I noticed that Nephi came out when the smell of the meat cooking was at its peak. I asked him if he'd had his vision, and he simply shook his head.

He ate, spoke a little to his favorite of Ishmael's daughters, then went back into his tent to pray through the night.

Eventually, several days later, he told us he got his answer. He explained all the parts of the dream that were interesting to him. Lemuel and I were bored, and I think Sam was, too, but we all sat there as Father had commanded, and listened to an explanation of the dream. It was from God, I knew it was, but it still made no sense to me.

19

Father prayed to God and got permission for the four of us, Sam, Nephi, Lemuel and I, to marry the daughters of Ishmael. Sam married Ruth, Lemuel married Esther, Nephi married Rachel and I married Naomi. I think Rachel was the least excited about the marriage, and Nephi pretended that he was doing what the Lord wanted, not what he wanted. He didn't smile about it or celebrate like the rest of us. I wasn't sure how that made Rachel feel, but she was the most sober of her sisters, so maybe it didn't matter to her. She and Nephi were a fine match.

Ishmael and Father negotiated over the contracts, which seemed foolish, considering the fact that he had decided to come to the wilderness in the first place because Father had sent us in search of wives. But we had to promise a whole list of things that we would do for our children to make sure that they lived well.

We had to educate them properly in Hebrew, and in reading and writing. We had to promise to never strike their daughters or if we did we would cut off our own hands. (Not sure exactly how we would do that, but it's what we promised anyway.) I would have promised to stand on my head for the rest of my life and to turn my whole body inside out if that was what it took to marry Naomi.

She was the water in the desert of my life. I didn't know that there could be someone who was so perfectly right for me. She wasn't what I had imagined a wife would be like. She was much more like me that I'd ever hoped for. She understood my jokes and she made me less afraid to be me. Somehow, she made me feel like I didn't have to worry about all the mistakes I'd made in the past or all the ways in which I wasn't Nephi. She didn't want Nephi. She wanted me.

It was a quadruple wedding, on the shores of the river, in the morning before it was too hot, though the sky was brilliantly blue and it felt like the whole world was singing for us. It turned out that was Ishmael's family, singing as the four daughters came out of their tent dressed in colorful silk robes. I don't know where they'd gotten them. I figured we'd seen everything they had to wear already. But it looked to me like someone—maybe Ishmael's wife—had packed wedding attire before they left Jerusalem.

Father presided over the ceremony. Because I was oldest, Naomi and I were married first. As the youngest, Nephi was last. We praised God for our good fortune, made so many promises I couldn't remember them all, and feasted on roasted meats and other delicacies that I'd been sure we would never taste again, fruits and cakes and even wine. It was in short supply, which was just as well as far as Father was concerned. He only had one glass and if he had any dreams from God that night, I didn't hear about them.

In the heat of the afternoon, we played in the river, ruining our finest clothes, kissing in full view of everyone, and then falling asleep on the sandy shore for a few hours until it was cool again. Then Father insisted that we listen to his scriptures. I don't know why, but he chose the reading for that day to be about Abraham saying that his wife was his sister to protect her. I did not want to think of Naomi as my sister, though Father said that we should all remember that we had to protect our wives above all else, that they were our most precious possessions.

"I'm not a possession," said Naomi, leaning close to whisper in my ear. "You remember that." When I didn't respond immediately, she began twisting my ear lobe until I yelped in pain. "Remember," she said.

"I remember," I yelped, and she let go of my ear.

She grinned at me then and kissed me. Sometimes when I was with Naomi, I didn't know which way was up anymore, except that she was always up. Father would have said that God should be my compass and that I should always follow Him, but Naomi had become my God.

In that evening, I got to take her to our own tent. It was made with parts of my tent and parts of the tent she shared with her sister. I think Ishmael's wife did that while we were being married. She had to have worked fast to do it with all four tents, though. Naomi liked it because she said she thought my tent was too small and she didn't like the idea of giving up everything she had had to become my wife.

We spent weeks in that valley, and then months. I kept expecting Nephi to tell us all it was time to move on and pack up. I figured that we had to be doing something wrong if we were so happy. We needed more hardship, more sorrow, more complaining. He was happy too, though, I think. His relationship with Rachel wasn't like mine with Naomi, but he adored her. I could see him watching her even during Father's endless scripture study each evening. He didn't touch her in public because he seemed to think that was inappropriate, but he memorized her in the dying light.

I thought that if Nephi could change and become more human, maybe I could be more spiritual. So I would get on my knees sometimes in the middle of the night, after Naomi was asleep. I would try to find words to speak to God. I would try to feel His presence near me, feel the warmth and love that I had felt only once or twice before.

Maybe I was too happy with Naomi. Maybe God was angry that I'd waited too long to try to pray. But there was nothing there. It seemed like God had disappeared.

I tried to go outside my tent and kneel by the river to pray, or go up to the rocks and look at the stars, hoping that acknowledging God's wondrous creations would help to know me better.

But God still did not speak to me. I certainly did not see Father's vision of the tree as Nephi had.

I saw nothing but the Jerusalem I had left behind in my mind. Maybe I was still back there, unable to listen to God because God wanted to move me forward. But if that was true, I was not the only one.

I noticed that Mother kept putting a hand to her stomach when she sat down and a hand to her back when she stood up. She was eating more and coming out of her tent less. I was pretty sure I knew what that meant, but hadn't said it aloud because it was too embarrassing, considering her age. And Father's. They had four grown sons old enough to have children of their own. And they were, well, I was sure Father would say that it was all according to God's commands.

20

Ishmael and Father argued long one evening about this very thing. Ishmael insisted that it was time to move on. He even accused Father of being afraid of leaving this place to go back to the desert. He said that Father was lazy and that God had ceased to speak to him. He also said that he had not left his whole life behind for this valley in the middle of nowhere. He wanted to go to the Promised Land.

"And if we expect to get there, we must start moving. God will tell us what direction we should go in. If we show him that we are willing to sacrifice and to work, He will guide our steps."

It sounded like the kind of thing that Father would have said to us, so I was surprised when Father contradicted Ishmael and told him, "There are times when God expects us to be patient and to wait for His words. If He wishes us to remain here, here we will remain until He tells us to move on. We do not tell God when we are ready for the Promised Land. He tells us."

Ishmael prayed rather loudly in front of the whole camp that night, but he finally went to bed.

The next morning, my father woke up before the rest of us. Another vision from God, I expect. He walked out of his tent and then started shouting.

If I hadn't been awake late into the night talking to Naomi about the possibility of having a child here in the wilderness, I would have been more interested in what he was saying. But I eventually got out of bed because Father was shouting so loudly that I couldn't sleep anymore.

I stumbled out of the tent and found Father holding a strange ball in his arms. It didn't look like anything I'd ever seen before, but it was clear that it had been made by a master craftsman. The metal was smooth and there was no sign of pounding. There were jewels all over it and a place that was flat and dark.

"It is from God. It gives us directions to the Promised Land!" Father exclaimed. "Can you see it?"

I stared at the dark spot, but I have to admit, I did not see any words on it at all.

"Nephi, tell them what it says!" said Father, pushing the ball of curious workmanship at Nephi.

As Nephi held it up, I was wondering how the ball had come to our camp. I would have thought we were completely alone in the wilderness. If someone had passed by our camp, why would they have left this for us without telling us who they were? It made no sense.

Unless the ball had been unearthed by a gentle wind in the night, and had been from a previous group that had once dwelt here. Which meant what? That God had led other people to this same place? Had they reached this Promised Land of His or had they died here? Were they unfaithful?

"It says that we are to head south and east," said Nephi. "For four days. To a land called Shazer." He handed the ball back to Father.

"Sam, do you see it?" asked Father.

Sam insisted that he had seen the same thing as Nephi.

I was confused. Why couldn't I read it and they could? Or were they lying to me and pretending that they could read it?

Eventually, Ishmael came out of his tent and looked at the ball, as well. He said that he could not read anything on it, but Father kept insisting that it was plain as day. None of Ishmael's children could read it, nor his wife. Mother said she could, but I didn't believe her.

Nephi and Father would tell us every morning what was written on the ball. Nephi mostly told us about the direction we were supposed to go in. He said that was what the spindles on the ball meant, but whenever I stared at them, the spindles seemed to shake all over the place. Sometimes I heard Ishmael's sons whispering about "magic" and "witchcraft."

Father, on the other hand, was always telling us that the ball had words written on it about the future. And they seemed pretty direct.

"Laman, it says that you will try to kill your brother Nephi," Father said. In front of the whole camp. "You must repent now for any evil in your heart, or any feelings of envy toward your brother. You know that the Lord loves him because he is righteous. You must love him, as well, or Satan will have your heart and will lead you to hell."

I bowed my head and murmured at Father that I would do my best. What I didn't tell him was that I had already tried to kill Nephi. Twice. Since we'd left Jerusalem, that is.

"Lemuel," Father went on. "The ball tells me that you will rebel against me even in the Promised Land and that a grave curse will be set upon you and your children for generations. You must bow your head and accept correction. You must learn to be obedient to me, for that is the only way that you can also learn to show obedience to God."

Lemuel went red in the face. I wished he would just mutter something to himself, but instead, he argued with Father in front of everyone. "No one can know the future," he said. "Not you and not even God. Certainly not that stupid ball. The future has not happened yet. It is unwritten."

"It is clearly written," said Father, pointing at the ball and smiling.

"Then why are you telling me to change?" asked Lemuel. "If the future were already decided upon, there would be no point in you trying to get me to alter it, would there?"

"I am trying to save your life, and possibly your soul, as well. I love you, my son," said Father. He looked suitably sad about the prospect of Lemuel's future.

"If I can be saved, then the ball will be wrong, won't it? And the ball can't be wrong, can it?" said Lemuel. "So there is no point in me doing anything other than what I would have done to begin with. Your ball has no power over me, Father!"

I knew what Lemuel was trying to do, and a part of me applauded it. The sons of Ishmael nodded to him and shook his hand later that morning in congratulations. We were all tired of being ruled by the ball. If we saw a good place to camp, Father had to consult the ball first. If it told us to keep going, we would keep going. If it told us to stop, even if there was no water, we stopped. No reason was ever given and while Father and Nephi were constantly saying why this place was the right one, or that place, I was pretty sure they were making it up as they went along.

We kept moving south-south-eastish and I thought we were getting closer to the Red Sea, but I couldn't see it. Neither Nephi nor Father mentioned it. I wished that they could use the ball to ask questions, but that didn't seem to be the way that it worked. It would be great if they decided they didn't like what it said, shook it up, and tried to read it again. Maybe it would say something different the second time?

I wondered if we all really knew what the future would bring us, would we try to do something different? Would we want to make it better? Or would we be so happy with what we saw coming that we'd race toward it? Maybe it depended entirely on if you were righteous, like Nephi, or not, like me. Every day was a struggle for me, because I was never sure if we were going to survive another day. Would we have food? Would animals attack us? Would raiders find us in the desert? Would another storm come?

Nephi never seemed to have these concerns. Nor Father, for that matter. It made me angry that they had it so easy. They just did what the ball said, and moved on. If I could have read the ball, maybe I could have done that, too.

No, I admit it. I couldn't because I didn't believe in the ball. I mean, I knew it was right there, but even if I could have read it, I wouldn't have trusted it. I didn't trust God, not Father and Nephi's God.

After all, their God was the one who had sent us after the Brass Plates from Laban. Sure, we'd been able to bring them back with us. But at what cost? We'd lost everything we owned of any value in Jerusalem. We had left behind a reputation that might make it impossible to ever go back. Nephi had killed a man. Even if he didn't face a trial in court about that, it must have changed him forever, which might be why he was following Father more now and not saying much about his own visions.

God had used us all and it seemed to me, had disappeared for weeks, then come back with a vengeance. God had power. I didn't doubt that. I just wasn't sure I wanted to be the man that God wanted me to be.

21

After we'd been traveling for two weeks along the river, the ball told us we had to veer away from it. Of course, this was a dangerous way to go and when Father read from the ball, Naomi and most of her sisters started complaining. We went without water for days and all we drank for several days was warm animal blood. If there was an oasis somewhere the animals were drinking from, we never found it. Every night, we went to bed thirsty and every morning we woke up more thirsty.

Ishmael begged Father to go back to the river, but Father insisted that he was following God's instructions on the ball. I thought Father might also be reminding Ishmael that he wasn't in charge and that he shouldn't have tried to get Father to move in the first place. I wondered if the ball would eventually tell us to go back to the river, but it didn't.

We kept going on, long past when I thought we would all wake up buried by sand and so desiccated no one would ever recognize us as human.

I thought that at some point, the thirst would be so normal that I'd stop feeling it, that I'd get used to it. But I can't say that I ever did. The first time I had to put my lips to an animal's neck and suck blood from its throat, I had to focus all my attention on not gagging and making that blood—and the animal's death—useless. The second time, it was the same thing. And the third time. It was never better.

Were our lives really worth the lives of so many other creatures? Was our quest to reach this mythical Promised Land so important?

"God has ordained this animal for our use," I heard Nephi say to Rachel. "It lived a good life, and now it has met the measure of its creation. It was happy to die for us. I saw that in its eyes."

"I'm with child," Naomi told me that night.

I'd guessed it for a couple of weeks, based on the way that she had stopped enjoying hunting. That night she hadn't offered to take her bow out at all, and watched as Nephi went out alone.

I should have gone out with Nephi anyway, to make sure that we had enough food, but Nephi's insistence on the ball being correct, and on us all following Father and God into oblivion, had annoyed me. If he had so much faith, let him hunt for us all.

Lemuel and Sam refused to go, as well. Ishmael's sons had long since given up doing any more moving than they absolutely had to. I think they might have been hoping that they died sooner rather than later. Or that not finding any animals to drink from would make Nephi and Father turn back.

So Nephi went alone that night, and brought back an ibex. The next night, it was another one. And on and on, big animals that shouldn't have been out here at all, that were clearly signs of a miracle from God. But it didn't make us eager to drink from them.

Though Naomi was carrying our child and I should have been thrilled at becoming a father, I had lost all the will to live. I got up and did what Nephi and Father told me the ball said to do. I was silent as I packed up our tent and silent as I trudged forward through the sand. Maybe that made their lives easier. Maybe that was why God had sent us to this forsaken place, so that I would learn humility and obedience at last.

I didn't dream about Jerusalem anymore. I didn't hope for something delicious to eat at the end of the day. It was just a matter of movement. This way, that way, up and down. And when I couldn't move anymore, then I lay down. And slept. It felt like death, that release of all my awareness. I began to look forward to death, not because I thought that I would see God then and be rewarded for a good life, but because death was the only rest I could imagine now.

Nephi began to collect blood so that he could bring it to us in our tents. He would drip blood into my and Naomi's mouths each night. I coughed on it, disgusted by the taste and angry that he was able to keep going despite all. But I didn't have the strength to choke it back up. It went down into my stomach, giving me enough strength to wake the next day.

I hated Nephi for that.

He was losing weight as we all were, even Mother and Naomi, who were with child. He looked worn and old. His skin was so tan now that it looked like it was leather. His muscles had faded away, leaving bones that looked too large underneath. He hadn't had much fat to begin with, but it was all gone now.

At least Rachel wasn't pregnant. I didn't hear them arguing. I didn't hear them speaking at all. I noticed several nights that Nephi was sleeping outside the tent, rather than inside it with her.

It seemed impossible to go on like this. What would happen when the babies came? How would the women give suck to them?

I didn't think anything could possibly get worse. And then Nephi's bow broke. He announced it after he had gone out hunting. He came back with nothing to feed us. I thought that we would simply lie there and die. I thought that I could finally have what I wanted, a true rest.

Ishmael's sons complained loudly about Nephi wanting us all to die.

I didn't say anything to defend him. My mouth just felt so dry. My lips had cracked so badly that I had stopped licking at them because they felt so hard. And not even blood seemed to trickle out of the wounds, as if my body was trying to keep all the fluid it could inside.

Somehow Ishmael's sons even had the strength to get to their feet and threaten Nephi.

He put up his hands and wept at them. I wasn't sure if it was because he was exhausted or just because he felt so guilty. Then he promised to try to make a new bow and arrow.

I had no idea how he was going to manage that, since the old one had been made of steel, but he did have some leftover parts of the animals from yesterday whose guts he could use for the string.

He ended up using some wood from a gift he had given Rachel for their wedding. He cut it down in the night, never sleeping, somehow feeling his way to the right shape without any light.

Maybe we should have cheered, but in the morning, we discovered that Father could no longer read the ball and his faith seemed gone, as well.

"We are going to die!" he exclaimed as he threw the ball to the sand. "We're all going to die here. God has deserted us. He has guided us to this place and then He has left us alone!"

"Father," Nephi said, trying to embrace him. "Don't speak like this."

Father shoved his beloved son to the ground. "Don't you tell me what to do! You are still my son and you will still obey me! I say we are going to die and that is what we are going to do! We are not going to take one more step into the desert on this foolish errand that I believed was God's will."

"Father, you must repent. Do not tempt God to punish us further," said Nephi. His voice was clear, but he spoke softly. Did he think that he was going to make Father feel better that way?

"I should never have taken us from Jerusalem. We could still be there now, in our beautiful home. We had so many luxurious things. We had servants who ate better than we have eaten in the last weeks. Servants of servants eat better than we do. Even the beggars in Jerusalem have better lives and are more favored of God than we!"

I had never heard Father talk like this. I'd heard him rave before, in the days before Nephi and Sam were born. But it wasn't angry or despairing. He had always been someone who was an optimist, even if there was no reason to be one. A crazy optimist. Even when he talked about the destruction of Jerusalem to people, it was always to tell them to repent, to change what was coming if they could.

"God gives us trials. All of us, even those who are faithful to Him. He knows that we learn and grow from struggles. If He took those away from His beloved, that would not be kindness, would it?" said Nephi.

"You are a fool!" said Father. "You cannot even let us die in peace!"

"We are not going to die!" Nephi insisted. "Father, you said I must obey you. I ask you to go into your tent and pray to God. I have a new bow. It is not as good as the first one, but if God blesses it, it will work even better than anything man has made. And I ask you for God's blessing. Ask Him where I am to go to find animals for meat. Ask Him and we will all eat again."

"Meat? We are tired of meat. We want to drink freely of a cool stream. We want fruit. And bread. We want sweets to delight us. We want tubers to roast and dip in oil. I cannot live on more meat and blood," said Father. But his voice was quiet as Nephi's now. He was tired of arguing, and perhaps a little ashamed.

Nephi waited for Father to go back into his tent, and then we all waited for Father to come out.

It was only an hour later and Father pointed north. "God says that He will have a herd waiting for you, and that He will make the bow work."

Nephi simply nodded and then headed out. A part of me told me to go with him. I could help him carry back the animals, at least. If we weren't walking today, I should have energy for that.

But I couldn't do it. I'd need his help to get to my feet, and I couldn't find the humility to call out to him and ask for help in front of everyone. It was different accepting help than it was asking for it.

We all waited in our tents as the sun rose and made us sweat, reminding us of our lack of water. Finally, as it was growing dark, Nephi appeared, dragging five animals after him. How he found the strength to do that, I will never know.

I ran to him then and helped him the rest of the way into the camp. Then people came eagerly and drank blood.

It was an important moment for us, I think. We stopped thinking of the hunted animals as something we could depend on. God could take them away from us anytime He wished. He expected us to show faith in Him, and we all said prayers that night thanking God for our lives, even if they weren't as comfortable as they had been in Jerusalem.

I was embarrassed to be reminded that if I were still in Jerusalem, I would not have Naomi at my side. I would not have a child coming in a few months, ready to call me Father. I would not have a chance to be a better father than I had had myself, something I had promised myself for many years that I would do.

"Thank you, God, for bringing us to the wilderness. Thank you for teaching us to be grateful for all that we have," I said quietly as I slipped into bed with Naomi that night and wrapped my arms tightly around her and the child.

Nephi continued to hunt for us, but we took turns after that going and helping him carry the animals home. His bow remained strong and we always found animals, almost as if they were waiting for us, or had been called by God to be just where Nephi knew they would be.

We seemed to be growing stronger, though I do not know how.

21

At last, we reached a place that Nephi called Nahom. There was a small stream there, though it was not always more than wet mud. Still, we were so glad to drink water when we could rather than blood. We stayed there for many days.

I tried to use Nephi's bow myself, but it would not work for me. Father insisted that the ball told us we were to move on, but none of the rest of us would obey him. I wondered if Father was glad for the rest, for he did not seem to be too eager to force us onward.

Then Ishmael died.

His wife and sons woke in his tent and there was much wailing, so that we knew something terrible had happened even before we saw his lifeless form brought out wrapped in his blankets.

It was a shock to me. I knew he was older, but somehow I had expected he would live forever. It was one of those moments in my life when I realized that we were all mortal. Even Father would one day soon die. And Mother.

Then Lemuel and I would be the oldest ones remaining. What if we hadn't reached the Promised Land by then? There was no way that we could return to Jerusalem now. I had no idea how to get there. We had to depend on the ball completely now.

Perhaps that was why that morning when I looked at it, I saw the words that Nephi said that he saw. Though later on, I questioned whether I truly saw anything, or was desperate, that day I was sure that God had spoken to me, that He loved me at least a little.

But Naomi and her sister and brothers and her mother were distraught over her father's death. They blamed Father for all the hardships we had been through. They said that he was crazy and more than that, he was ego-ma-niacal. All this travel in the wilderness hadn't been about God. It had been about Father getting people to follow him and feeling like he mattered, when in Jerusalem he had been nothing.

They said some very cruel things about his past, some things that I didn't even know about before. People he had supposedly cheated and lied to who had believed him for a little while. People who had followed him and then dis-appeared mysteriously.

I had to stand with Naomi, but I wasn't sure that every-thing they said was true. Father simply said that if they would repent, they would be able to read the ball. He said that Ishmael had died because God had decided that he was not worthy to go any further with us to the Promised Land. That did not go over well.

For several days, Ishmael's family refused to move from the camp we were at. It wasn't a particularly good spot, but they were stubborn. Father threatened every morning to go on without them, but then claimed that the ball told him to stay. I didn't know what was the truth. I didn't even ask Father to see the ball because I thought that would be a betrayal of Naomi and her family on its own.

Then there was a terrible sandstorm and Father claimed that it was because we were being unrighteous and that the ball could not help us.

"Do you want to die here in the desert? Or do you want to trust in God's servant to continue to guide you in the way of righteousness and safety in the Lord?" he demanded as we all tried to dig out from the sand covering what remained of our camp.

At that point, it wasn't as much to do with following God as it was to do with following anyone anywhere away from this place.

My son was born as we were still in the wilderness. I didn't know where it was and once we were gone, it didn't matter anymore. That evening, after we had pitched our tent, Naomi began her labors. I called for her sisters to come to her, which was what she told me she wanted. Rachel still had wine, and she brought it with her to help dull Naomi's senses.

Normally, men stay out of the tent during childbirth, and I tried to follow tradition, but when I heard Naomi crying out in pain, I went back in. Her sisters were helping her to squat. She did not need me there, I think. But I needed to be there. I held her hand and felt her press her pain into me. She broke at least one of my fingers and we laughed about that later. At the time, I was eager to share in her pain and when I got a first glimpse of my son, I cried out as she did.

He was red and tiny and squawling and I suppose there was nothing about him that made him look any different from any other infant. Yet to me he was beautiful. The most beautiful person I had ever seen. I looked into his face once and knew my life was changed forever.

I will never forget his face, eyes holding my gaze, expecting everything from me. I thought I understood life anew. I understood my father and his terror at the expectations Lemuel and I had from him. No wonder he had run away from that. What man could feel he was sufficient to those expectations. Naomi and I named him Lehi, after Father, and I never regretted that choice. He was a reminder of all my father had done wrong and that I would do better.

"I will never abandon you," I promised my small son Lehi, as I held him and the women dealt with the afterbirth and cleaning up Naomi. "I swear to you, I will never leave you alone. I will never turn away from you in fear. I will be with you in all things."

I was weeping by the time Naomi asked to put our son to her breasts to suckle him. She teased me about being a baby myself, and I did not care. This was the happiest day of my life. I told her over and over again how much I loved her, more than life itself, more than anything I could imagine. I told her that I would do anything for her, that I was sorry for her pain.

And then in the morning, we packed up again and Naomi had to walk. It was cruel and I wanted to shout at Nephi that he should understand that a woman needed to rest after giving birth. But he would only say that the ball had told him to move on. It was always the ball, and God, and never his own choice.

A few weeks later, it was Mother's turn to give birth. I had watched her growing larger and wondered if she would be able to stand up day after day. But somehow, with Father's help, she kept up with the rest of us, following the commandments of the ball.

That night, Naomi left the baby with me and went with her sisters to help Mother in her need. I could hear my mother crying out and went to stand with my father outside the tent. He had been through this four times before, but he did not seem to be any calmer about it than I had been.

"She is too old. I should not have asked this of her. I should have kept away from her," said Father.

Those were the very things I had thought of many times in the last nine months.

But Nephi joined us then and said, "It was not you who chose for her to be with child in her old age, but God. It is a miracle, like Abraham's wife Sarah. God will succor her as he did Sarah, and she will be strong in labor."

Father patted Nephi's back and seemed pleased with these words.

In the morning, the child had still not been born, however, and Mother was past crying out her pain. She was too weak for that.

Naomi came out and told me in whispers that it was time for us to prepare Father to say goodbye, that there was nothing more they could do to save Mother.

When I tried to tell Father, he shook me off and told me I had no faith. He turned to Nephi and asked him to pray to God for Mother. Nephi did this, of course, and insisted that Mother would be well, and that Father would have not only a fifth son, but a sixth, in the future.

I wanted to strangle Nephi with my bare hands for saying this. If Mother survived, she would hear of this and feel obliged to give Father that sixth son. What a burden for her to carry at this age! And Nephi said that he loved her?

It was in the heat of the day that Mother was finally delivered of a fifth son, whom Father said was to be called Jacob. He was born the wrong color and was not breathing, but Naomi pressed her own mouth to his lips and pressed life into him. Then he breathed and we could all hear his cry, which echoed throughout the camp.

It was then that Nephi went to consult the ball. He told Father that it said we were to go north again that day.

I feared what would happen if Father went into that tent full of women and told them they must pack up and be ready to continue on their journey without any rest, and with Mother in the state she was in.

Instead, he told Nephi, "God will forgive us for resting today." He would not listen to Nephi the rest of the day, but went into the tent and sat with his wife. He brought out the child for us all to see, held him up high. I could see pride in my father's face, but also fear.

He would not leave the camp the next day, nor for another week. He waited until Mother was ready to go on and said so, and even then, he stayed with her, holding the child with his own hands, at the back of our group. I thought well of my father for the first time in many months then, and believed that he had learned to be unselfish in the wilderness.

Then it was Rachel's time to give birth. She was clearly in labor pains at the end of one day's journey. I told Naomi, who told me that she did not need my help to know when her sister needed assistance. But Rachel sent Naomi away, and in the morning, she packed her tent and walked again, still clearly in pain. There was no baby born that night, and Nephi prayed mightily to God to relieve his wife's pain.

That morning, Rachel tried to walk with us, but fell back, and then simply dropped to the sand. Nephi called out a stop to all of us, and we pitched tents in the middle of the day.

Naomi went in to help Rachel, but was sent away.

"What is it?" I asked.

"The baby is upside down," she told me. "I am afraid for my sister and for the child."

She and the other sisters tried to turn the baby, but it was too late. The child was already deeply engaged.

Nephi prayed more loudly and Father tried to console him that this must be God's will. Nephi shouted at him and said that his child would live.

Two days later, Rachel was delivered of a daughter. Both lived, perhaps only through Nephi's constant prayers over them and care for them. If I had ever doubted that Nephi loved Rachel or that he was a man like other men, this was my proof.

Ruth had a daughter, and then it was Esther's turn. Lemuel had a son, and his boy was enormous, as big as some children six months after birth. Yet Esther was up again hours later, ready to travel with us.

Mother was pregnant again only months after Jacob's birth, according to Nephi's word. Father was alternately proud and terrified of the coming birth, but the second time, Mother did better. Naomi and her sisters made sure to keep her well fed before the birth and they gave her advice on exercises to do to make herself stronger.

It worked, because Joseph, my father's second son in the wilderness, was born without much trouble. He was hale and hearty and I could only think about how wonderful it was that my father now had a third family in his old age. His new sons had made him more mellow than he had been before, and I liked the new man he was now. I came to think of him as a friend, almost.

We kept traveling east, according to Nephi's reading of the ball. Nephi was in charge again, though all of us had to depend on the ball or we would die. God had brought us to this point, where there was no choice for survival but through faith.

22

We kept traveling until we reached the sea. Nephi called it Irreantum, which meant "Many Waters." It was so wonderful to be near the water again. We couldn't drink the salty water of the sea, but there were many streams and rivers nearby that ran into it. The taste of water after so much blood was delicious to me, and I praised the Lord every day for that.

Instead of animal meat, we ate fish, usually roasted because we were so tired of having to eat raw meat for the sake of our traveling. We were finally able to plant some of the seeds that Ishmael's family had brought with them when they first came out of Jerusalem. It was difficult by then to remember Jerusalem at all. It felt like a dream I'd had. A wonderful dream, but impossible.

Our clothes were all in tatters, but we mended them again and again. We started to use blankets to make clothing for the children, though sometimes they went about naked. No one cared about that anymore.

It had been eight years, according to Nephi, since we left Jerusalem, but I frankly had lost count. I didn't even know the day my son had been born, not in terms of a day to remember. He and the other children were thriving near the sea and Naomi had begun to grow strong again. She didn't use her bow and arrow much anymore, but she challenged everyone in the camp to races or competitions whenever she could.

Once at Irreantum, Father stopped talking about the Promised Land and the ball stopped working, or at least telling him where we were to go next. We were in a good place. We were comfortable in our own way. Even Nephi stopped pressing us forward. We read the scriptures, but not every day, and Nephi stopped telling us all what was right and wrong. I think he was happy with his daughter, too. She was a pretty little thing, even if I thought she spoke too much.

If I thought sometimes about the children of Israel under Moses, and how they had all had to die before their children could enter the Promised Land, I did not care. Let my children have whatever it was that God had in store for them. I was not worthy of more than this, and I accepted that. I was happy in what God had given me.

After some years by the sea, Nephi woke one morning early and disappeared. I saw him only because I was out doing my own business before returning to the tent to cuddle with my wife before the children woke. I did not ask him where he was going, but he did not return for many days. When he did return, there was a fire in his eyes that I remembered from many years ago.

"What's going on?" I asked him.

"God has commanded me to build a ship," he said in that low, prophetic tone I recognized.

This all over again? "A ship? You cannot have heard Him correctly," I tried. Why would any of us want to leave this place God had brought us to? If there was a Promised Land beyond this one, how could it be worth all the trouble to get there?

"We must have a ship big enough to hold all of us in order to cross the sea and arrive in the Promised Land," Nephi said. "God has told me that He is tired of waiting for us to ask Him for the next step. He is pushing us forward. He has shown me what the Promised Land is like, and I am eager to get there."

He wanted to be able to act as our ruler again, I thought. He had to use God for that. "No one will follow you," I warned him.

"They will if they ask God for a vision of The Promised Land. Anyone who sees it would do anything to get there," he said confidently. He looked young again somehow, like a little child telling about a dream from the night before.

I paused a moment and thought about how to stop him from doing this. It was ridiculous and utterly impractical. "How are you going to build a ship? We have no tools for that." Neither Father nor Ishmael had imagined a sea voyage.

We might be able to find enough wood around here from trees that grew around the rivers to build a small dingy or something, but a ship large enough for all of us? We were more than sixty people now. And a ship that was safe enough to cross the ocean? None of us could build something seaworthy, and I wasn't going to trust the lives of all my family, including Mother and Father, to one of Nephi's experiments.

Nephi insisted, "God has shown me where to go to find ore to smelt into tools. And He has shown me in my mind a pattern of the ship I must build."

Right, good. We were starting from ore. How long did Nephi think this would take? How many ships would he have to practice on before he made one any of the rest of us were willing to board?

"And did God also tell you how long it would take to get to the Promised Land?" Were we all supposed to get on without knowing if we would ever get off?

"God has told me as much as I need to know for now," said Nephi.

Faithful, blessed, perfect Nephi once more. He didn't need to ask questions. He didn't need to worry about his family's survival. God protected him and always had. But I wasn't convinced.

"If you pray to God, He will give you confirmation that this is His plan for us," said Nephi. "And perhaps He will even share the pattern with you, so that you can help."

Unfortunately, I had already tried this thing with God and that wasn't the way it worked, not for me, anyway. If God had really wanted someone who knew what they were doing when it came to building, He would have come for me in the first place, not Nephi. But apparently God wanted a complete beginner for some reason. Or just someone who wasn't me.

Lemuel came over about that time and started asking about the first tool that Nephi had smelted. It looked pretty rough to me. I suppose it would function as a hammer, but it wasn't the kind of tool that we would have used in Jerusalem when I was into building.

"That's what God told you to make?" said Lemuel. "That's going to make a ship we're supposed to ride over the ocean on?" He shook his head. "No. Not me and my wife and children."

"If you helped me, then it would be finished much more quickly," said Nephi. "And we would be on our way to the Promised Land."

"Help you make tools like this?" Lemuel laughed. "No thanks. I have better things to do with my time."

Sam came over and watched us. He didn't participate one way or the other, but I thought it said plenty he didn't defend Nephi.

Nephi started to use his tool on some pieces of wood he'd found. Whatever it was he was making, it looked nothing like a ship at the moment.

"I'm not getting in any ship that you build with that tool," I declared. "And neither will anyone else. Even Father and Mother wouldn't get into a ship built by someone with no experience at all. You'll kill us all."

In the last eight years, Father had made Jacob and Joseph into the new Nephi and Sam. They were petted and cared for so that they hardly did anything for themselves. Sometimes I wondered if this irritated Nephi at all, that Father did not think of him as the favored son anymore. He always wanted the small ones who were impressionable and obedient, and Nephi wasn't like that anymore.

Nephi said, "Moses led our ancestors out of Egypt. He opened the Red Sea for them and saved their lives when they would have died at the hands of the Egyptians. He called down manna from heaven for them. He brought them commandments so that they could learn the ways of God."

We could argue about how many of those problems were Moses' fault to begin with, but all right. What was the point Nephi was trying to make here? Was he supposed to be Moses?

"And when their children were ready to enter the Promised Land, God gave them strength to destroy those people who were already living there. God knew the path and every step that it would take to move from Egypt to Israel. If not for God, our ancestors would be slaves still. And you think to convince me that I should turn my back on His words?" said Nephi.

Maybe I was telling him to do just that, when God was asking the impossible. Or maybe all I wanted was for God to speak to me sometimes, to tell me that I could be like Moses.

"There are miracles and then there are miracles!" said Lemuel. "I can believe in Moses, but not in you, Nephi."

"God has already ensured that we survived the impossible journey to Irreantum. Why can you not believe that He can bring us one step further?" asked Nephi.

Lemuel shook his head. "Fine. You build your ship. You can put your wife and daughter on it. Take them to the Promised Land without us. We're happy here."

"God has commanded me that I must bring all of you with me. I cannot go alone!" said Nephi.

So he did need us, after all. I was surprised to hear him admit this. He couldn't go to the Promised Land without us because he needed to do some empire-building. He had to be in charge of us, and that didn't work if we opted out of the whole adventure to begin with.

"Then I guess you're stuck here with us," said Lemuel cruelly.

"You will come with me! You will assist me in the building of this ship!" said Nephi. He was shaking with fury, or so it seemed to me.

"Right. Yeah. That's exactly what we're going to do," said Lemuel. "Try and make us!"

"You will do what God has decreed and what I have foreseen. I have seen us all in the Promised Land. With our wives and children, building a new city there. I have seen it!" Nephi's hands had tightened into fists and his face had turned a dark reddish color. I was actually afraid for him for a moment, that he might burst out of his skin, or stop his own heart with his trembling.

"I hate the Promised Land!" said Lemuel. "And I hate God! Nearly as much as I hate you!" He threw himself at Nephi then and the force of the impact threw them both on the ground. I watched as they grappled with each other, kicking and grunting, neither one showing any clear advantage.

Honestly, I'd expected Nephi to win in any physical combat with Lemuel. Where was God?

"Laman, come help me!" heaved Lemuel. "Pin him down so we can beat him to death!"

I stepped forward to help, though I had no intention of doing what Lemuel was suggesting. I couldn't face Father, for one thing. Let alone God. I wanted to separate them, that was all.

"Laman!" Nephi called. "You know that God speaks to me. Help me!"

I stepped back. This was tiresome. I had to do enough negotiating between children's arguments at my own house. I didn't need to do it with my brothers.

"Laman's on my side!" Lemuel called out, moving away from Nephi and reaching out to me. I took his hand, meaning only to pull him to his feet.

To my shock, Lemuel used the weight of my body to fling me against Nephi. My breath was knocked out of me and for a long moment, I couldn't move.

That was precisely when Nephi seemed to magically float to the air. He seemed literally to be standing a foot above the sand and he glowed. Like a lantern. Like a lamp back in Jerusalem. Like a tree that was about to be struck by lightning.

He held out a hand to both of us. "You will repent and obey me. I command you in the name of God to stop fighting against me and to aid me in the building of this ship."

His voice wasn't just prophetic. It sounded like it came straight from the heavens, like he was Moses himself.

"Damn you, Nephi!" said Lemuel, who was looking rather worse for wear. Whatever he had done to Nephi, our brother was healed now. Whereas Lemuel's face was bleeding and bruised and it looked like he was missing a tooth. He could only get to his feet with a limp.

"Touch me and I will show you the power of God which I can use against you any time that I choose. For God has given me the keys to use His power on earth when I see it is necessary to further His aims."

"Touch you? Is this some kind of a trick?" asked Lemuel. He glanced up at me.

I wasn't going to touch him. I'd already seen enough to know that God was with him. God didn't have to send angels to protect my younger brother anymore. Nephi was now trusted to use that power himself.

Lemuel tried to run at Nephi, barreling at him with his head.

And he landed on his backside. Worse than that, there was a smell in the air as if he had become burned meat.

I leaned over Lemuel and offered him a hand, but he seemed too stunned to recognize me. His mouth opened and closed around words.

"We will help you build the ship!" I said to Nephi. I held my hands up in defensive posture. I had never meant to be on Lemuel's side in this, though I could see why Nephi might interpret it that way. I hadn't been on his side, either, had I?

"I know you will! I know because I trust in the power of God which I hold," said Nephi.

Well, he could act a little more grateful. But of course he thought he did it all himself.

"What do you want us to do, then?" I asked.

Lemuel was still moaning. I would explain the details to him later. When he wasn't so angry. Or so much in pain.

"I need wood," said Nephi. "Will you two cut wood from nearby trees and bring it here?"

"But it has to cure first," I said. I knew that from my work on buildings in Jerusalem. "You can't use green wood because it will dry and all your joints will be ruined."

"God will make it work without curing it," said Nephi.

Hmm. Or maybe God expected me to explain things to Nephi at this point.

"We'll get the wood cut and started curing," I said. "Tomorrow." Lemuel would take that long to recover and I couldn't haul the wood here by myself.

Nephi sighed. "Tomorrow, then," he said, as if he was being very tolerant.

Now that I was roped in, I knew I would do everything I could to make sure that this ship was sturdy enough to get us wherever on the planet that God—or Nephi—had planned for us. I had to make sure that my family survived this.

I went back to my tent that night and tried to explain to Naomi what had happened, but she was livid. She didn't want to leave Irreantum.

"Do you want us all to die on that ship?" she demanded.

"No, of course not," I said. "That's why I want to be part of the construction."

"Everything your brother Nephi is in charge of turns out horrible for everyone but him," said Naomi. "You've seen that. I know you have."

Yes, but I'd also seen Nephi manifest the power of God when Lemuel tried to attack him. I'd seen an angel. I'd watched us all survive things that should have killed us in the desert.

"I thought I'd married a man," she said.

"I am a man. I'm trying to do what's right here, Naomi," I said. "As lovely as this place is, you know it isn't a place we can build our homes."

"I don't know that at all!" She waved a hand. "We'd be perfectly happy here. Why not use those tools Nephi is making and that wood for a city?"

"We don't know where we are. We don't know if there are any ways for us to trade with others here. Will we be able to continue to feed a growing city?" I asked.

"Better than wherever Nephi wants to take us," Naomi complained.

"I promise you, I'll make sure the ship is soundly built. No one will get on it if I don't trust it to last through a long voyage," I said. I was begging her to listen to me.

"And if I won't get on it anyway? And I won't bring the children?" she asked.

I didn't know what to say then. "I love you, Naomi," I said.

"Then you must stand against your brother at some point," she said.

At some point, but not yet.

23

After that, Lemuel and I helped Nephi with the ship every day after that. It was hard work, and the worst of it all was hearing Nephi tell us every step as if we were stupid, small children who could not understand anything. I knew how to build much better than Nephi. But he told me everything I did was wrong according to the revelations he was getting from God.

"You have to get him to listen to you," Naomi had insisted when I tried to explain my problems to her. "You are the older brother. You have more knowledge in this matter."

I knew that I did, but Nephi would not listen. "God has told me how to build this ship, not you. If this ship is to arrive in the Promised Land safely, I must listen in every particular," he said when I approached him the next day.

"Have you ever considered that God might want you to listen to the people around you who already have knowledge about certain things?" I asked. God might not think much of me when it came to visions and scripture reading, but surely God had seen that I had been good at building.

"God wants me to learn everything anew. He has told me that I must forget everything that I think I know and trust in Him utterly. Otherwise, I will not be able to learn the full truth He has waiting for me," said Nephi, his chin held high.

"He wants to teach you anew, but that does not mean to forget all the knowledge that centuries of human experience have given us," I said. Why did Nephi always have to be the one who was the teacher, and not the student?

"Human knowledge is nothing as compared to God's knowledge," said Nephi. And he told me again to cut the wood his way, to cure it his way, and to use the wooden pegs his way to link each piece together.

I could not help but complain to Lemuel when Nephi was gone. I couldn't complain to Naomi because she would just tell me to stop helping him and I knew I couldn't do that.

"He thinks he knows everything. He says he is the humblest man in the world because he's ready for God to teach him, but he won't listen to anyone else," I said.

"Sometimes I hope that this stupid ship will sink the moment we all get on it, just to spite him," said Lemuel.

I smiled a little at that. "If it sinks, then let's hope it's close to shore so we can all swim back."

"Yes. And we'll watch the ship slowly sink into the ocean while cheering."

"And Nephi will be running around telling us that we don't have enough faith," I said. "If we had more faith, we'd be able to keep the ship afloat."

"Because faith solves every problem," said Lemuel.

Jacob and Joseph were still so young that they couldn't help much in real ship-building. But Nephi went out of his way to pretend to include them. He didn't have to worry about them getting hit when we moved a piece of wood or getting splinters from wood that hadn't been sanded or getting fingers cut off when we were using a saw, because he was directing things now, and getting revelation from God about new tools he needed to smelt.

I tried to tell Mother what was going on, and point out that this was dangerous. But these days, Mother slept a lot of the time and when she wasn't in her tent, she just waved her hand and told me that I should worry less.

"We may all die here. Why should we try to make our lives worse with contention than they already are?" she said.

I went to Father after I gave up with Mother. He only came out of the tent to eat, and I wondered if he slept at all at night, based on how tired he looked.

"Has God told you about the Promised Land? About the ship?" I asked.

He shook his head. "God loves Nephi better than He loves me," said Father. "I am a tired, old man, not much use anymore. And I have made too many mistakes in my life."

"But you've repented of them." I thought Father had always said that if you repented to God, then it was as if you had never done them. You were clean, weren't you?

"I tried to repent, but my evil habits keep returning to me. Nephi has nothing of that sort to hold him back. He is young and vigorous and God can teach him everything that is necessary. I will let Nephi teach Jacob and Joseph, as well." He waved a hand at the world and closed his eyes.

I put a hand on him and shook him gently. "Father, you had a vision. God told you to bring us into the wilderness. You are the one who sent us back to get the Brass Plates. You told Nephi that he could do it, if he had enough faith."

"God did what he had to do with me. But He does not need me anymore. It is time for a new generation to follow His words."

I shook my head and went out of the tent. I didn't tell Lemuel what had happened, but I admit, it was difficult not to sympathize with the sons of Ishmael when they complained about the work Nephi made them do during the day. Nephi had them stoking fires, cutting wood, and dragging it to the ship building site. We were all doing exactly what he told us to do.

Much sooner than I'd thought possible, the ship was staring to take shape. Jacob and Joseph would sometimes spend the evenings running through the deck and below, finding hiding places and pretending that they were already on the high seas. Nephi would go up to them when it was dark and he could no longer work on the ship itself. He would tell them stories about their forefathers in Egypt, about the creation of the world, and about Laban and the Brass Plates.

Somehow, Nephi tended to forget the part about him killing Laban. He would skip straight from bringing Laban all of our most precious items from the house in Jerusalem, and go straight to coming back to the wilderness with the Plates and Father blessing him for his faith.

Then there came the day when I pointed out that we needed separate storage for our food on the voyage. Nephi had not thought of that. He spent the next whole day, walking around the ship, praying here and there on his knees, and apparently getting no answer. Finally, he went up to the mountains where he had gone before. He was gone for three straight days.

The sons of Ishmael had already begun to plan to take the ship back to Jerusalem when Nephi returned with new tools and explained how he would build storage into the shape of the ship already. It was ingenious, I admit. It was almost as if the ship had been planned for that storage in the first place. I guess it was. There was no denying that God must be helping Nephi with all of this, because he certainly could not have done it on his own. He just didn't know anything about it.

I tried to feel the love of God in this. He must love me if He cared enough to make sure the ship I was on was safe for me and my family, if He had included me in the group to leave Jerusalem and be saved. I was going to the Promised Land. My son would have the Brass Plates to learn from. He would have all the things I had not had when I was young, that I had always resented Nephi for having.

But God didn't love me enough to send me my own vision, to use me to build this ship.

"Do you think that God will ever send a commandment just to me?" I asked Nephi late one night, when Jacob and Joseph were asleep on the ship and Lemuel had gone back to his tent.

"If He sent one to you, would you obey it without question?" asked Nephi.

"Without any question at all? Is that what you did when God told you to kill Laban?" I poked at that sore spot because I knew it was there, and because I felt very exposed at the moment. I could hear the waves of the sea against the shore nearby, and the birds calling out overhead. I could feel the bulk of the mountain overhead, stopping most of the winds from beating at us.

"No," said Nephi. "I had a moment of doubt then," he said.

"Was he shouting at you? Struggling?" I asked, trying to picture the scene in my mind.

"No. He was drunk. He was snoring loudly on the side of the road."

"And you took his own sword and cut off his head."

"I had never killed anyone before." I could hear the strain in Nephi's voice. He took no pride in what he had done.

"So you told God you didn't want to?" I wondered, if Nephi had said no and simply walked away, would we be without the Brass Plates? Or would God have been forced to try someone else? Might I have had a dream then, and the next day, or the next? When Laban was drunk again, maybe I would have been the one to find him in the street and I would have been told to kill him. Would I have hesitated as much as Nephi had? And would my eagerness to kill have made me a better servant of God—or a worse one?

"It's a commandment. The second set of commandments Moses brought down from Mount Sinai, because the others were too difficult. These were the easy commandments. Do not kill. Simple."

"But God told you to disobey that commandment." What did this mean about God? What kind of a being was He, that He used a man like my father, a drunkard, to send dreams to because my father believed them? And acted upon them? What did it mean that he used the younger son like Nephi, untaught except in the scriptures, strong in body but uncertain in so many other ways?

"He said that it was better for one man to die than for a whole nation to dwindle in unbelief."

"A whole nation? You mean our children?" Would they be a nation in the future? It was hard for me to grasp that vision. But God had not sent it to me.

"If only he had taken our jewels and all our precious things. He could have had his life, as well." Nephi sounded sorrowful, not proud.

"Until the city was destroyed," I pointed out. Nephi still believed that it would be—or that it had been already in the years since we'd been back.

"Yes, until then."

"Do you hate God for making you kill a man, then?" I asked. Nephi had spent the last eight years with the rest of us, not asking God for visions. Until recently, anyway.

"I could never hate God," said Nephi, tears in his eyes. "But I hate that Laban forced me to kill him. I hate the evil in Laban's heart that made him care more about the value of the Brass Plates in coin than in their value in changing the hearts and lives of others. I hate the sin and the greed in him that made him see us only in terms of what we could give him instead of what we could have offered him."

I took that in for a moment. Then I realized what Nephi was saying. "You think that God would have offered to let Laban come with us. If he'd asked. If he'd given us the plates and then said he believed that Jerusalem was going to be destroyed." He could have come instead of Ishmael. Laban had many daughters and sons, as well. Was Ishmael God's back up plan?

"I would have welcomed him as my brother," said Nephi.

I was Nephi's brother, but I could believe Nephi wouldn't care about blood relations. "Well, I think Laban was odious," I said. "He thought too highly of himself. He would have made this whole trip unbearable. He would have thought he was in charge of everything."

The difference between me and Nephi was that I wouldn't have been bothered much by killing Laban. I wouldn't have liked the messiness of it, the spray of blood in the moment, and the effort it took to wield the sword that way. But the guilt—I would never have felt that. Nephi did. And that was why God had chosen him. Because he wouldn't have killed gladly. Because it wasn't easy for him.

24

Finally, the ship was finished. It was truly incredible. The size was unlike anything I had ever seen, even on the docks in Jerusalem. That was partly because this ship was not yet in the water and partly because I had built it. The wood was oiled and shone in the desert sun. The color was golden and seemed like a gift to make up for all the things we had lost when we left Jerusalem. This was what I had spent my life to become: a ship builder. It seemed a good trade.

I brought Naomi out to look at it, so that she could see that her fears were ungrounded. She'd refused to come out and look at it in any of the other stages and had continued to insist that she and our children were not going to board it.

"Hmmph," she said. But I could see she was impressed.

"It's well-built," I said. "There's no reason to be afraid of traveling on it. I think we're safer on that ship than here by the sea. We'd be better off weathering a storm there than here. And there aren't any dangerous animals to worry about there."

Naomi had killed a sandcat only a few days ago, saving the lives of our son and Nephi's daughter, as well. She'd done it with her bare hands because she'd left her bow and arrow in the tent and there was no time to go back for it.

"And you are to get no credit for this?" she asked. "You are a builder, Laman."

"I've never built a ship," I said.

"Your God has no respect for you," she said.

I bowed my head. I knew she was right. "Do you wish you'd married Nephi instead?" I asked in a low voice.

She laughed heartily at that. "Nephi? No. He was always too young for me, too unformed. I would have dominated him completely. You are the man I love, Laman. But I want to see you demand more for yourself. You deserve it."

She must be the only person who thought so. "I will build us a home when we reach the Promised Land," I promised. "It will be the envy of all."

"You will build more than our home," Naomi insisted. "You will build all the buildings there."

"Yes," I said. And to myself thought—unless God decides He wants them built in some new way that only Nephi can listen to.

I noticed that for once even the sons of Ishmael stopped their complaining about Nephi, Father's dream, and leaving Jerusalem.

We were all ready to go as soon as Nephi said the word.

He announced to everyone that we would be boarding at the end of the week, and that we needed to pack enough to sustain us for a journey of three months. It seemed impossible to me, but we packed what we could.

Naomi and Ishmael's other daughters packed the precious seeds from the plants we had been living off of. We didn't bother to pack our tents or more clothes than one change. There was a lot of mending and patching from clothing we would not bring with us. Naomi went hunting to dry meat to bring with us and I dried what fruit I could. The other sisters baked until we were all salivating for the chance to get on the ship.

I prayed to God and tried to express my gratitude. For the ship, but for everything else, as well. For the chance to be here, with my family, for Naomi and my children, for God's tender care over us in the past eight years, even for Nephi and for my father's dreams. I felt as if God came down and put His arms around me in a firm embrace, a welcome home.

At last, we woke and boarded the ship. There was much weeping. Father had argued with Nephi about staying at Irreantum because he was too old, but Nephi insisted he must come. Mother would not come out of her tent without weeping and wailing because she did not want to go through more hardship.

Nephi made sure that Laman and I carried Mother aboard and showed her to her sumptuous room. She seemed content then, though the ship had not begun to move through the waters yet. Father stood with Nephi on the deck of the ship to see the moment when we were launched.

Nephi had made sure that each family had separate quarters, which made for less arguing. Naomi was pleased with our room, and so were Rachel and Esther.

Ishmael's wife and sons, however, were angry. Though the sons were grown, they had to share space with their mother. I had a bad feeling when I saw their faces, that this was going to come back and bite Nephi later on in the journey. But there was nothing he could do about it now. The ship was built and it was time to launch it.

Three months, he'd said it would take to get to the Promised Land. Compared to the eight years we'd already spent in the wilderness and the year building the ship, it shouldn't have seemed like that long. But we were all going to be in one vessel. No one could go off on his own (or her own) and go hunting. We were going to be in each other's way constantly.

We celebrated that evening with feasting and food and plenty of wine. Naomi told me that she wanted another child, and I did my best for her on that count.

But the next morning when I woke, I could hear a lot of wretching. We were hardly away from shore, but there were more than a dozen figures by the side, uncomfortable with the movement of the ship.

It was going to get a lot worse than this when we got out onto the open water, I knew, but I refrained from telling anyone. I'd heard far too many stories from soldiers of those who died on board because they could simply not get used to it and starved to death. They were buried in the water itself, no matter how much they hated it.

Nephi was kneeling at the bow of the ship, holding in his hands the ball, the Liahona, that I hadn't seen for months. I guess it made sense that Nephi hadn't needed to use it, since we hadn't moved anywhere since we got to the sea. And the ball apparently didn't have the ability to tell him enough information about how to build a ship. Not that I had been able to read much on it anyway.

"God says that we are to lay our course due east!" Nephi proclaimed, when he got to his feet. He held out the ball for everyone to look at. As if that would make any difference to the rest of us.

"There's a storm out there!" said one of the sons of Ishmael, pointing to the clouds just past us, right on the horizon. "We should go around it."

"God has already decided. We go east. If there is a storm, there is a storm and God will get us through it," said Nephi.

Well, he never did try to win any popularity contests, did he? I loved Nephi. After working with him on the ship, I had even come to respect him. He had an open heart. I could see why God found him useful, because he could be turned easily any way. He seemed to have no opinions of his own to get out of the way. It made him vulnerable and in that moment, I felt protective to him as an older brother.

"Could you ask again?" I said quietly to Nephi as he came close enough to steer the ship.

"I have already asked and God already answered," said Nephi. "If someone else wants to ask, God will give the same answer, I am quite sure."

So we headed east, and we went right into the storm. It wasn't a light summer shower, either. We hadn't kept track of the seasons very well since we arrived at the sea, so I didn't know if it was fall or spring, but it was some massive change of weather, and this summer was bringing it with.

We couldn't stay on the deck or we'd be drenched within minutes. Only Nephi stayed up so he could keep the ship on course—a course he stubbornly refused to change.

The rest of us were down in our quarters, and being so tightly pressed together for so long did not do good things for the moods of anyone. Our wives began to complain that the children were too noisy. The children complained that they were bored, and began to fight with each other.

"Do something!" Naomi urged me when young Lehi got into an argument with Lemuel's daughters.

I slapped young Lehi and the girls, which got me into trouble with Lemuel, who told me I should only punish my own son. We almost came to blows, but our wives kept us away from each other. At least they did during that storm.

And on top of all of this, everything stank of vomit because no one dared to go to the deck of the ship to relieve themselves when they grew ill at the sudden movements that the storm created. We were all sick in one form or another. I began to suspect that Naomi was expecting another child, but she had never been this sick before with the others.

Father and Mother did not come out of the quarters, but when I went into them, I could see that they were both seriously ill. I helped them for a few hours. Then Naomi came to relieve me.

"There is more going on here than a storm," she said.

"What do you mean?"

"It's a plague. Everyone is sick, and it's not just the sea. We brought it with us from Irreantum."

"A disease?" I asked.

She nodded. She knew about sickness better than I did.

"We were without illness for eight years," I pointed out. I hadn't even noticed that fact until now. Though we had all been weak from lack of water and having to drink animal blood and raw meat, we had never had fevers or other symptoms.

"And now we are not. Your God has withdrawn his protection from us," she said.

"My God?" She was Jewish as much as I was.

"I mean that He speaks to your family in a way He never speaks to anyone I know but the prophets in the scriptures. Laman, I do not like Nephi, you know that. But he may be the only one who can save us."

I nodded to her and tried to get some sleep, but the sons of Ishmael would not stop threatening Nephi's life. They were sure that it was the fault of the storm that we were all ill. They did not believe in Nephi's prophecies, even though they were on a ship he had made with God's help.

25

On the third day of the storm, I went up to speak to Nephi because the others were threatening to throw him overboard and take the ship to the nearest land they could find, no matter where that was. They could sell the ship and use the earnings to gain passage back to Jerusalem. Or hire a proper crew to pilot it. Once Nephi was gone, that is.

Even Father and Mother had begun to doubt.

Naomi told me I must go speak to Nephi. "He must pray and ask God for mercy. We cannot bear this," she said.

So I went, hating the arrows of rain striking my face and the terrifying height of the waves all around the ship. How could Nephi stand to be in the midst of this without any help?

I stumbled forward, nearly going overboard twice. But at last, I was close enough that he could hear me.

"We are near death, Nephi. We need to go around this storm!" I shouted at him.

He turned to look at me, his arms wrapped around himself, shivering. "This is the direction God commands us to go. There must be a reason for it."

"And there is a reason not to go this direction, as well. Nephi, I warn you. If you do not get us out of this storm, there will be a rebellion against you."

"God will protect me against that, as well," said Nephi stubbornly.

"Nephi, please. You don't know what it's like down there." I waved at below decks. Nephi's wife and daughter were as ill as the rest of us, and he had not even seen them.

Nephi stared at me for a long moment. "God will protect us all as we follow Him," he said.

So we were suffering because we weren't following God? What more did God expect of us after all we'd been through? We got on this ship, didn't we? After eight years in the wilderness?

"Let me take over for a little while," I suggested. Nephi didn't look well and he couldn't have slept in days. "Go sleep. Spend time with your wife and daughter."

Nephi swallowed hard and looked away. "I cannot do that. I must stay."

"Nephi, trust me. You tell me what direction to go in, and I will steer the ship. I swear it," I said. I was lying, and I was lying with great fervor. I did not know if I would fool Nephi or not.

"Promise me that you will steer east," said Nephi. He held up the ball to my face. I could see the spindle pointing east, even if I could not read any of the words.

"I promise," I said, already feeling relief.

"Swear it on the lives of your own children. For if you steer wrong, you will be risking their very lives," said Nephi seriously.

I hesitated.

"I will not go, then. I cannot go if you will not swear it to me, Laman," he said.

He was a fool! As bad as our father had ever been— worse than him, in fact. "I can't protect you from the others if you continue in this foolishness," I said. I'd done as much as I could to protect him already, and did he care? No. He saw only that I was weak and unfaithful.

"The foolishness is yours, and anyone's who does not follow God," said Nephi, his jaw tightening as he gripped the steering of the ship.

Perhaps if I got Father, Nephi would listen. But I wasn't sure I dared to bring him out in this storm.

Nephi leaned over and folded his arms. He closed his eyes and began to pray, standing up as he was, still steering the ship. I couldn't tell what he said, but by some coincidence, the storm looked now as if it were actually lessening in intensity. The rain wasn't as severe and I could see a few points of light in the clouds.

I went down and reported this to the others, and then told them that Nephi would not leave the deck or let anyone else take control of the steering of the ship.

"It's the eye of the storm!" said Lemuel. "That means nothing. We are only halfway through. We may not survive another week of this!"

"We should wait," I said. I looked for Naomi and she nodded her approval.

I went to sleep that night, sure that I had averted the coming clash between Nephi and the others.

But they went up while I was sleeping and began to attack Nephi.

Naomi heard the noises first, and shook me awake. "Go and save your stupid brother!" she said, and pointed upward.

I hurried up just in time to save Nephi by binding him tightly with rope and gagging him with a rag stuffed in his mouth as the others threatened to kill him. He had no sense of self-preservation and kept shouting out threats of what would happen if he was taken off the deck.

"God will cause this ship to be thrown into the depths of the sea, never to be seen again! God will raise a sea serpent to swallow us as Jonah was swallowed by a whale! God will send pestilence and an angel with a fiery sword!"

I couldn't tell how much of this was his own opinion and how much of it was God's, but Nephi did not sound entirely sane to me, not anymore. His eyes were wide and he was hot to the touch, which made no sense, considering how wet and cold the storm was. He was trembling in the ropes, and I felt him fall to the ground.

"He is ill!" I finally said, as he vomited, then closed his eyes and seemed lost to the world. I touched his throat to feel him still breathing, but it was shallow. He was not well. "Let me take him to his wife," I begged.

But the others refused to let him go anywhere. They wanted him to suffer, and they wanted to be sure that he could not convince anyone else that he was right. So they kept him there on the deck, so sick that I think it was a mercy of a kind, since he did not remember all of it.

One thing I cannot deny, however, and that was that as soon as the sons of Ishmael began to steer the ship, the storm grew worse. Lemuel insisted that it was just us going back through what we had passed before, but I did not believe it was true.

I saw the ball in Nephi's hands. The spindle had gone haywire, twitching this way and that or sometimes spinning around and around without stopping.

When he came to himself several days later, Nephi begged me to set him free, to let him take control of the ship again. "I don't care what happens to me. But set us going east. If you do that, the ball will work again. You can throw me overboard, but pay attention to the ball, Laman. Get my wife and daughter to the Promised Land,

and Mother and Father. Get Jacob and Joseph safely to shore, and teach them from the Brass Plates. Promise me."

He was not even angry with me, after all I had done against him.

"I cannot read the ball. You know that."

"Then Father will read it," said Nephi. "Or Jacob or Joseph. God will choose one of them. He does not want us all to die."

"Perhaps He does want that," I said sullenly. "If He wanted us to live, He would end this storm." If God had power to do such a thing, which I was beginning to doubt, despite my previous experiences. An angel was one thing. A shock was of the same kind. But storms were something else.

"Tell them you will be reasonable. They might let you go then," I said. "Be humble with them." Nephi knew how to be humble, why not with someone other than God?

He shook his head. "I will tell them I will steer the ship as God commands, which will lead us to safety," Nephi said.

Needless to say, this was not effective in making the others want to give control back to him.

We were two more days at sea, and one of the sons of Ishmael was swept overboard and never seen again. His family wailed and mourned. The rest of us were so ill we could barely move. Our food was all sodden or rotten and inedible. We could not catch any fish, and the water we had brought on board fresh was contaminated now with salt from the ocean. We were all going to die.

The remaining sons of Ishmael wanted to throw Nephi overboard as their last living act. Lemuel voted with them. Rachel pleaded with her brothers for Nephi's life, but I think it was Naomi's harsh words to them that made them soften. She told them that they were cowards and that they were jealous of Nephi. She also told them that she would tell any children they ever had what they had done and make them call them cowards, as well.

They bowed their heads to Naomi and told her she and I could go to Nephi and loosen his bonds, no more.

Lemuel acted as a go-between and told Nephi that he would set the ship to the course Nephi told him to.

But when Nephi looked at the ball, he shook his head. "It won't work. We have been too wicked. God will not allow the ball to show anything until I am set free. I wish it were not so, but that is what He has spoken to me in my dreams here in bonds."

"We must set him completely free," Naomi told me, but I shook my head. I wasn't sure we could get her brothers to do that.

Again, she worked on them night and day, threatening them, pleading with them, making them laugh at stories of their childhoods together, and telling them of a dream she had of the Promised Land and the life that was waiting for us there.

It was another full day before they allowed her to set him free, but when they did, retreating from the steering, the ball began working again.

Then Nephi dragged himself upright, and with Jacob holding him up on one side and Joseph on the other, he began to steer the ship.

The storm stopped immediately. I had never seen anything like that, before or since. No one could say that we were headed toward a calm spot in any case. The clouds were black overhead, pouring rain upon us, the ship tossing this way and that. The next moment, the clouds were gone, and the ship was quiet as a lamb.

I heard retching, but no other sounds. No birds, no rush of waves against the wood of the ship, no cries that we were about to die.

Father and Mother praised God for our deliverance, as did Naomi and a few of the others, including Nephi and Jacob and Joseph.

I embraced Naomi and thanked God that He had sent her to be my wife.

"Don't thank your God for that. I chose to be your wife because of my own good sense," said Naomi. "I know what kind of man you are, Laman, and I know you are worthy of my love."

It was the kindest thing she could have said to me.

I heard many mutterings about the difficulty of what we had been commanded to do. But all of Ishmael's remaining sons and Lemuel eventually went below to sleep the first uninterrupted sleep in weeks.

Miraculously, the food dried out and what had been rotten was fresh again. The water was made unsalted, and we began to be able to catch fish and cook it on the deck. Slowly, we recovered, and no one else was lost but the one son of Ishmael.

"Now you have to make sure this doesn't happen again," Naomi coaxed me two days later. "Go speak to your brother and get him to understand how to be more politic with the others. If he is going to rule over us in the Promised Land, he needs to learn persuasion rather than ordering."

She was right, as it seems that she so often was. So I went to Nephi in an attempt to reconcile with him.

"You must learn to speak more wisely," I said. "Try to mold your words into what others want to hear. Push them gently in one direction, and then again. Do not try to move them all at once."

Nephi shook his head. "You do not understand, Laman. I do not choose the words I speak. God chooses them for me."

"But surely you can decide how to present them," I suggested.

"And if I did that, God would not speak to me anymore," said Nephi. "I would be as you are, Laman. Is that what you want for me? For God to think of me as He thinks of you?"

It stung me, and I walked away. Perhaps Nephi had lessons still to learn, as well.

26

We saw land a month later, in the morning. In fact, Jacob saw it first, because he and Joseph were the only two people Nephi trusted to follow the commands on the ball as he did, and so one of the three of them had to be on deck at all times, day or night.

Jacob called out to the rest of us, "The Promised Land! It's here! I see it!" He pointed and leaped for joy.

We were all shouting soon, excited that we had finished the long journey at last. Naomi had given birth only days before to our second son, whom we had chosen to name Nephi, and I had to help her stand on the deck so that she could see what we saw. I held the baby in my arms and made sure that he could see the land, as well.

"This is where you will live. You will be happy here. You will have your own children, and you will bury me in the earth one day. You won't think of Jerusalem or deserts in your life. You will have plentiful food and never need to drink blood. You will help build a city here. More than a city, a kingdom."

A feeling came over me as I spoke that this was the truth, that God was speaking through me in a blessing to my son. It was the first time in my life I had experienced anything like that. I'd heard God speak through Nephi and through Father, but it was so different when it was my mouth He used. It felt like I was as tall as a mountain, like my voice was strong as thunder. I could feel His presence in every part of my body, trembling and tingling.

And when it was gone, I felt weak as a baby myself.

"Laman?" asked Naomi.

"I'm fine," I said, smiling at her to allay her fears. "I need to speak to Nephi, that's all."

My arms trembling, I had to give young Nephi back to Naomi. I called Joseph to take Naomi back below. Had I done enough to gain God's favor at last? I hoped and prayed for it, and slowly, my strength returned.

It took three more days for us to reach the shore that we had seen that first day, and during that time, almost everyone stayed on deck, even during the night. It was dark and we could see nothing of the shore then, but we could feel it there before us.

The winds had changed and the taste of the air was different. Instead of simply salt and fish in our noses, we could smell plants and fruit, even other creatures with flesh and blood. It had been so long since any of us had eaten something fresh that we could hardly bear the thought of waiting even longer.

Finally, the day came that the ship shuddered to a stop. Two months after beginning our journey on the other shore, we were home. This was the Promised Land.

It was completely different from the place we had left. There was no sand here, no desert heat. The ground was filled with all manner of vegetation, underfoot and overhead. It was the most beautiful place I had ever seen. I could hear the bees buzzing everywhere around us, so it was indeed flowing with honey. There were flowers of such color that my eyes hurt to look at them. The animals were so tame that they waited for us patiently, as curious as children.

Father was the first one to step off the ship and onto the land. Trees were all around him, and in a moment, he was no longer visible to us.

"Father!" called Nephi.

"I'm here. At last, in the Promised Land," called Father back to us.

Then we were all scrambling down to the shore, leaving the ship behind.

I could not help but think that there were things we would have to unload. All the seeds the children of Ishmael had so carefully brought with them, our tattered clothing that was all that we had to wear. But it felt as if we did not need any of that. This land was bursting with food ready for us to take, and we would not need anything from the ship. The land would be sufficient for all our needs.

I held baby Nephi while Naomi called the other children to her and held their hands as we climbed down. I had already felt the ship stop, but to feel the ground under my feet was such a change that I swayed on my feet for a moment, trying to adjust properly to the lack of motion. The children managed the change more easily, and ran ahead of us, laughing and playing with the very animals that we had seen waiting for us.

Surely God had brought us here, I thought. Again, I felt a wave of His presence fill me and testify to me that I was blessed by His hand, that this was where we were meant to come. After all of our troubles, we were at last home, to the place that He had prepared for us. We would never want for anything again. All our disputations were over. God would be over us here, and how could we complain against God Himself?

Once I was under cover of the trees, I couldn't see the ship. It felt as if we were in another world, not simply another land. I could almost forget about the ocean crossing and even Jerusalem. We were here now and nothing else mattered.

As we walked through the jungle, I could hear Nephi calling out now and again to keep us close together. It was a good thing, because we could have easily been lost. And this land was so vast that we could have searched all of our lives for each other and never had success, if we went in the wrong direction for just a day or two.

We found a freshwater stream, and then we were all along the rocky banks, smiling and laughing.

Naomi and I kissed and then she threw mud at my face and I did the same to her.

The adults acted as much like children as the little ones did. We splashed in the water naked, chased one another, danced to improvised music made from sticks hit against tree trunks. We shared fruit that was hanging off the trees, sweet and delicious.

I held Naomi's hand and wept with her as our children explored the land around us entirely without fear.

Soon, we were clearing land to make a camp. Naomi gave baby Nephi to her sister Rachel and was as strong as any of the men.

A few hours later, as we ate and sat together with tall tree branches as our shelter overhead, I remembered then the dream that Father had had about the fruit, white and delicious above all other things, he'd said. And that there was an iron rod to guide us to the tree, and a river of dirty water to confuse us, and a building in the sky where the voices of others mocked us for going to the tree.

Father had worried that Lemuel and I would not make it to the tree, but here we were, at his side. He had not lost anyone, except the one son of Ishmael who had gone overboard. But no one spoke of him anymore, not even Naomi. It was as if he had never been. His wickedness had received its reward, which was that he had no place even in our memories.

I had struggled many times to obey Father and Nephi when they told us to do things that made no sense. We had made mistakes. We had argued and we had tied Nephi up. We had refused to pay attention to the ball, and been unable to read the words on it. But somehow, here we were, even so.

God had given me Naomi, and my sons and my daughter. We were in a land of plenty. What else could any man ask for?

It was a perfect day. I suppose one can only expect one perfect day in a lifetime.

It did not last long enough.

27

The sun fell from the sky in the Promised Land as surely as it did in any other place, and in the night, we huddled together by the river we had found, not because it was cold, but only because the darkness brought new fears. We could hear animals calling out in the distance, and we did not know if they were as friendly as the ones we had already seen.

"I should get my bow," said Naomi.

"Not now," I told her, holding her hand tightly in my own. I did not want her to risk the journey back to the ship alone.

The night seemed endless. My stomach began to growl, and then the pains hit me. I had eaten too much of the fresh fruit at once. Or so I thought at first. When I could no longer stand, or make sounds, or do anything but writhe in agony on the ground, I began to be sure that the fruit was poisoned.

Naomi soon was as ill as I was. Only the children seemed less affected by the stomach pangs. I tried to vomit, but it was of no use.

I sweated and counted the moments of life and wished I was back on the ship once more.

Then I heard Nephi's voice clear as day around me. "We thank thee, God, for our safe arrival here in the Promised Land. We thank thee for the lives of our children and our wives, which thou has kept safe in thine hand. We thank thee for this bountiful new land, which we will soon learn to understand. We thank thee for the promise of thy son in the future, who will come to redeem all our sins, all our ills, all our pains."

I heard him begin to vomit then, and I thought his prayer was over, but I was wrong.

He thanked God for the delicious fruit we had eaten (and which he did not mention had poisoned us), for the trees that were over our heads to keep us warm, for the water we could hear around us, for the animals that were so plentiful here, and then he prayed for the strength in the morning to begin a city. He asked for God's help in finding the proper place to begin building the first dwelling, and he said that he would begin first to build a temple so that we could offer our thanks and sacrifices to God all the day long for the rest of our lives.

At first, I wished I could laugh at him, but I had no energy for that. And then I wanted him to shut up and go to sleep, because my stomach had stopped hurting just enough that I thought I might be able to manage that for a little while. My first sleep on solid ground in months.

In the end, I did sleep, though when I woke, Nephi was still praying loudly and I did not think he had stopped. I wondered idly what would happen to the ball, the Liahona that Nephi had relied on for so long for directions. It must still be on the ship, but we wouldn't need it here.

Then the sun rose and it was light again, and though I never recaptured quite that first day's glory in this new world's perfection, the sounds of the animals receded and we followed Nephi as he guided us through the jungle and toward a mountain. It was only later that I realized we had become so used to following Nephi that we hadn't noticed that he wasn't using the ball and probably had no better idea than any of the rest of us where we should go.

"This is where I will build the temple," Nephi declared, standing in the middle of the clearing and holding his arms straight to heaven.

Lemuel and I and the sons of Ishmael all started to stake out our own claims to the land around the temple. Nephi could build a temple first. The rest of us were going to build our own homes. It might not be Jerusalem again, but it would be as like it as we could manage.

"This will be your city," Naomi said happily. She and I spent hours every night, planning out our own home and the other buildings I would make. At last, it felt like I would be able to show what I could do, what I knew best. Even Nephi would have to see how good I was at this.

"If we never have to sleep a night in a tent or a ship again, I won't complain," said Naomi wearily. She put her arms around me and held me tight. She smelled sweet, even if we hadn't bathed fully in months. She smelled like happiness and peace. The children swirled around our feet, then the little one cried for me to pick him up, so I did, and held him tightly between me and Naomi.

"We made it," I said. "To the Promised Land."

"We did," she said, and kissed me. "I'm so happy. Are you happy?"

"If I'm with you, I'm happy," I said, full of gratitude to God—and even to Nephi. Without Nephi's dream of going back to Jerusalem for Ishmael and his daughters, I wouldn't have Naomi or our children, the greatest parts of my life. Nephi might have been selfish in wanting a wife to end his loneliness, but he'd asked God when I would never have thought to.

During the storm on the ship, my greatest fear had been that Naomi and the children would die, and that I could not save them. We were safe now. We would never be in danger like that again. And I could also thank God—and Nephi—for that.

I started work on our home immediately, going out to edge of the jungle to cut down trees. That would widen the area of the clearing, and it seemed to me that would be a good thing. Lemuel and Sam and the sons of Ishmael were also cutting trees and clearing land to build homes, but not Nephi. Nephi was dedicated to his idea of building a temple, and he looked for stone to build it with because he said that stone would last much longer.

First, he had to find where the best stone for building was in the area. He prayed about that, of course, and God gave him an answer. Then he had to figure out how to cut it on his own, and carry it to this place. That was a thorny problem, which he solved by finding animals he could use to pull for him.

He kept asking if anyone wanted to help him, if we wanted to earn blessings from God for our work on the temple. Each morning and each night, he prayed at the temple site as his family lived under a makeshift tent.

I felt sorry for Rachel and the little girl, but when I looked at her one night, Rachel said, "You will not build a house for her when her husband won't do it himself."

"Why not?" I asked, wondering if this was a jealousy between the sisters I'd never seen before.

"It will be wasted work. Nephi won't thank you for anything you do. Even if you help him with the temple, he will take all the credit, as he did with the ship," said Naomi as she kneaded bread from grain she had planted and grown in the few months we'd been here.

"Is credit what really matters?" I asked.

"Yes, it is," Naomi insisted. "Rachel married him because he is the prophet. You think she doesn't remind us all of that, every day? Esther and I married the lesser brothers, the miserable ones, the ones God has left untouched by His glory."

"Is that the way she puts it?" I said, getting a little angry now myself.

"She doesn't want to be comfortable. She wants to be proud of herself and her husband. If you built her a home, you would take all that away from her and she wouldn't thank you for it."

I looked at Rachel again. She stood with her back very straight, but I found it hard to believe she was enjoying living under the trees like that. But Rachel might be right about her not being grateful if I built her a home.

"What do you think I should work on, after I've finished our home, then?" I asked.

"Well, Jacob and Joseph will need homes eventually," said Naomi. "They're old enough to marry. And then our children will be old enough to marry, as well."

I looked at young Lehi and young Nephi and had a hard time imagining them old enough to marry. But she was right. The time was coming and I'd best get used to the idea of them leaving our home for their own.

"And then there are other buildings you could work on. I know Nephi is building a temple, but what about a church for weekly services? What about a building for a government? At some point, we're going to need civic leaders. You could run for office." She looked at my slyly.

I thought about how I'd managed to keep Nephi alive on the ship when everyone else wanted to kill him. I'd done a difficult thing in a difficult situation. I'd been able

---

to see both sides. Maybe I would be good at government, after all. I'd frankly rather build, but if Nephi was the other choice, I could see why most people might prefer me. It wasn't that I was wise or good or endowed by God on high. It was only that I was like the others, and they'd trust me to think of them rather than God's word.

"What about the ship?" I asked. I'd noticed that someone was taking wood from it, making it impossible for it to go out to sea again. I wasn't sure that was a problem, but I'd noticed that it was happening.

"Who cares about that? Anyone who uses wood that's already been put to a test like that storm deserves what they get," said Naomi with a wave of her hand.

"You don't think we should keep it intact, just in case?" I asked.

Her eyebrows rose. "You think any of us will go back into that thing for any reason?" she asked.

"What if it turns out there are dangers here we don't know about yet?" I was thinking out loud.

She laughed. "Then we can travel further south. Or north. On foot. Not on a ship that nearly killed us all."

It had saved us, too, but I didn't remind her of that. The idea of going back to those closed quarters was hard for me to think about, too.

"What if we can't get along?" I asked. "Or if Nephi decides that he has to go back to Jerusalem to get something else he forgot?"

Naomi kissed me gently on the forehead. "I'm sure that there will be factions here. People will move away from us for other reasons, too. They'll want different land to grow food on, or more space for bigger buildings. Or to get away from Nephi and his calls to repentance. But they won't do it on a ship. We're here now and there's no going back. Not even for Nephi."

I wasn't as sure about that as she was, but if she was right, I wondered if I should take down all the wood from the ship so that no one was tempted to try to go anywhere on a ship that might not be viable now.

"There will be businesses we need to make space for. Bakeries and markets and racing arenas," said Naomi.

"That seems a long way off," I said, glancing out at what was mostly still jungle here.

"Not as long as you might think," said Naomi.

I had never thought of her as ambitious, but I suppose she was, at least for her sons.

She went on, "We could have a library with books that everyone could read. Your father needed the Brass Plates desperately, but he doesn't share them. If we taught one of our children how to copy them and then allowed them to be lent out, think how that would change their futures. Everyone could read and write, not just the special children chosen by their parents."

Not just Nephi's children, was what she meant. And why shouldn't my children learn to read and write? Why shouldn't they know what was on the Plates of Brass? It wasn't as if Nephi had gone back to get them all by himself. Laman and Sam and I had been there, too. We had suffered and sacrificed for God. Our children should reap the rewards of that.

We had the first version of our house finished by the end of that month. I helped build a home for Mother and Father after that, who had been living with Sam and Ruth, while Jacob and Joseph were living with Lemuel and Esther. Once their home was finished, I started on a church building, as Naomi had suggested.

Nephi's temple foundation was big enough to fit a thousand people, or so it looked to me. I had no idea why he thought a temple would need so much space, but I ignored him as I'd become used to doing. The church was smaller and less grand than what he was planning, but I wasn't sure his temple would be finished before he died. And then what? Did he think his son would continue building it when he still had no home?

When winter came, it was mild, but the growing season was over and I was glad that Naomi had been wise enough to set aside a good amount of food. I brought some to Rachel and her daughter, who were still without a roof over their heads. If she was taking pleasure in Nephi's temple, I couldn't see any sign of it.

Despite Naomi's warnings, I couldn't bear to see them without a home of any kind. They were the only ones left who had nothing, so I began to build a modest two-room home for them.

Naomi had been right that Rachel would not thank me for it. She moved in even before it was finished and bothered me about a hundred different improvements she thought I should complete for her, though she never offered payment. She took it as her due, it seemed.

As for Nephi, he didn't notice what I'd done, either. I think he slept most nights on the temple grounds and only went home to his family occasionally. How he survived I don't know. God must have fed him as with manna from heaven, because I don't think Nephi paid any attention to what his body needed. He kept hauling stone through the winter and only fed the animals because they would not work for him otherwise.

When the growing season came again, Naomi made new bows and arrows for the hunters so that we had plenty of meat. I worked on more buildings to increase the size of the city. As Naomi had warned, Jacob and Joseph begged me for homes of their own and offered to trade me just about anything, including a chance to look at the Brass Plates and to learn to read them and copy them for the library I had in mind.

Father and Mother did not come out of their home often, and I had to check in on them myself to make sure that they had food and water. Some days they were entirely lucid and Father would call me to repentance or chastise me for old sins that he remembered more clearly than I did. Other days, both Mother and Father were confused and did not remember that we had ever left Jerusalem. Mother wanted to know where her best silks were and why the servants did not come when she called. Father wanted more wine or to tell me about the scriptures, though I had little time for that.

I got into the habit of sending young Nephi and young Lehi over to visit each evening, so that they were not alone, but Naomi tried to make sure that our sons were prepared that they might one day find that one or both had died—and that it would not be their fault.

My parents, dead. My father, gone to the God he had spent the latter part of his life serving. It seemed incomprehensible to me. We were here in this strange new land because of my father's dreams, but he had no more dreams now. He muttered to himself as if he was speaking to an invisible someone at his side, but there was no sense in it.

I went to ask Nephi if he wished to say goodbye to Mother and Father before they died, a warning that the time was coming soon. I had to repeat my words several times before he understood what I was saying, but even then he had no interest in the project.

"I am working on the temple. I am sure that is what my parents would have me do," he insisted.

"The temple will still be here to build when they are gone," I reminded him.

Nephi was angry at this. I think some part of him must have known that he was neglecting his other obligations. "Father taught me to be a man of God," he said, standing up to prove to me once more than he was taller than I was, though no longer as muscular as he had been when he had built the ship.

I went away from him shaking my head and wondering if God would always choose to speak to those who were so single-minded. I found I did not envy Nephi as I once had. What did he have that I should envy him for?

But it was only a few days later that Nephi stopped work on the temple for two weeks because he said that God had revealed to him that he must begin to make his own plates, with his own records in them like the Brass Plates we had brought from Laban. He began to call the children for daily lessons in reading and scripture study as Father once had.

"You see what he is doing?" said Naomi when I came home one night and our boys were acting out a scene from the scriptures that Nephi had read to them.

"What?"

"He saw your idea of the library and could not bear not to be the origin of that idea. He has to take it over for himself," she said.

But what did I care about that? "It suits him better than it suits me," I reminded her. I'd had so little of the learning that Nephi had.

"But now everyone, including our own sons, will remember the library as his legacy," Naomi complained.

I shrugged. I did not care about credit in the way that she did. So long as our sons were taught about their history. We were in a land so far from home that they might never meet any other Israelites. I didn't know if there were any people who already lived in the Promised Land, but if there were, they were far from this place.

We had another child, a daughter, that year, and Naomi asked me to expand the house by another room. Instead, I built an entirely new house for our family, and when it was finished, I invited Rachel to move in to the home we had left behind.

"She won't do it. She's too proud to take something I've abandoned," Naomi predicted.

But not only was Naomi wrong, but I heard Rachel thank me for the first time when I helped her move in her things.

"This room will be Nephi's," she said, and gestured to the room farthest from her own. "He won't be here much, but he will insist on having his own room so that he can sleep well."

I waited to see if she would complain anymore about him, but what she said was, "I have been talking to your mother more often these last months."

"Oh?"

"She says that your father was very much like Nephi. He was a great man."

"Yes, a great man," I said, pitying her.

"The temple is very beautiful, don't you think?" She looked out at it.

It was a beautiful building, I will admit. Perhaps not quite the match of the temple in Jerusalem, but far better than any of our homes. It was something that he could be proud of, something his children would brag about for generation after generation.

The stones were perfectly cut and the first level was nearly finished, something I was not sure Nephi would ever live to see. He was building far faster with the stone than I'd have thought possible for a single man working almost entirely on his own. His son went to help him sometimes, but he was too small to lift very much, and I think Nephi mostly told him more scripture stories than lessons about stonework.

Nephi's temple would last far longer than our simple homes made of stone. But I had only ever intended for them to last as long as we did. In this damp jungle climate, everything rotted but stone, and when Nephi spoke of the coming Messiah, I knew that he imagined that Christ Himself would come to this temple, long after he was dead and gone, and that it would be the only thing we had ever built that would be suitable for such an occasion.

Once, I might have been angry at Nephi for taking all the glory to himself, but it didn't bother me now. Let him have the glory of the ages. I had my wife and children. I was happy.

28

"You must go see your father," Naomi told me one day after she had visited my parents.

"Why?"

"He is dying," she said.

"He has been dying ever since we arrived here in the Promised Land," I said.

"Yes, but he has been dying slowly before. Now he is dying quickly," she said.

I hurried over and realized that she was right. Father could not stand up out of bed and he was blind. He only recognized me by smell.

"Laman," he said.

"Yes, Father, I'm here."

"I love you," he said to my surprise.

I thought by then he might have mixed me up with Nephi or Sam. But I said in return, "I love you, too, Father."

"No, Laman. Listen to me. I have always loved you. You are my first born. Do you understand?"

I felt a wave of emotion then. "Yes, Father," I choked out. "I have sons of my own now." Though I loved them equally, young Lehi had been the first. He had made me a father and there was a special bond with him because of that.

"I was afraid that I was not a good father. That was why I went away. I was ashamed of myself," he said in such a low tone that I had to lean in close to hear what he was saying.

"You came back," I pointed out.

"Yes, and then I believed that you and Lemuel were lost to me. I had two new sons so that I could be a fine father to them, and I put all my hopes and expectations on them," said Father, holding my hand tightly.

"They are good sons," I said. "They follow the Lord." Lemuel and I hadn't done that, not in the beginning, anyway.

"And Joseph and Jacob," said Father. "But I should not have blamed you and Lemuel for who you were. I should have taught you better. I should have . . . " he drifted off and for a moment, I thought he had gone to sleep. Then he began to weep.

"It was too late by then. We wouldn't have listened to you," I said. It was true.

He gasped. "I made Nephi a ruler over you. I never thought of giving you or Lemuel a chance."

I snorted at this. "Father, Nephi was the one who was having visions from God. Of course, he was the one to lead us." I could say that now without any feeling of rancor about it.

"But now you are—you are doing so much for the family here. For the whole community."

"Father, I could never have done what Nephi did. Building a ship, getting the Brass Plates. If it were up to me, we never would have left Jerusalem, and if we had, we certainly would still be in Irreantum." I still had fond memories of that place, still dreamed of it, though this Promised Land was in many ways better. I had been happy there for the first time in my life.

"His temple," said Father in a dubious tone.

"It is a monument to his God," I said. "If you could see it now, you would know why it matters to him so much." I had no doubt that God had given Nephi a vision of the finished temple to sustain him, and the rest of us would have to wait to see why it was worth so much effort.

"Do you forgive me, then?" asked Father.

"Father, there is nothing to forgive," I said. I didn't want to weep with him, not at the end like this.

"I was a miserable father, Laman. Please forgive me for that."

I was weeping now and could barely speak. I got out, "I forgive you, Father."

"And if you forgive me, I hope that you can forgive Nephi," he said.

"Nephi?" I asked. I found that I didn't want to talk about my brother.

"He has done what God has asked him to do. He might have done it more gently, or with more understanding, but he brought us here."

"Yes," I admitted. "He did."

"Then can you forgive him for thinking himself above you?"

Putting it like that made a knot inside of me unwind. He had put himself above us and Father acknowledging it made it easy for me to nod my head. "I forgive him," I said.

Father let out a long breath. "Thank you, Laman. You are a good and worthy son. Remember that."

I wept more.

"Laman, I fear for the future. I fear that you and your brothers will argue and that there will be a terrible schism. Promise me that you will hold fast to Nephi and the others, that you will keep the family together, no matter what it takes."

I didn't know how I would do this, but I was already starting to build a government. I suppose that I could try to make sure that Nephi had some say in it, though it didn't seem he wanted anything like that. Maybe Rachel would make her voice heard? Or Jacob and Joseph could speak for Nephi's family and their own.

"I will try, Father," I said.

"Laman, I trust you to do this. You are the eldest son. This is your responsibility."

"Yes, Father," I said.

He held my hand for a few more moments, then fell asleep. I stayed with him, and when he woke, he asked for Nephi.

Mother was outside the room, talking to Naomi, when I emerged. She looked so beautiful to me that I almost forgot how old she was. She had always been a beautiful woman. No wonder so many men had tried to marry her once Father had abandoned us.

"Has he made his peace with you?" she asked me, holding my gaze.

I nodded.

Her hair had gone entirely white, and there was not much left of it, though she coiled it around her head and pinned it on top. Her teeth were yellowed, the ones that were left, but her voice was as steady as ever.

"Good. It has weighed on him for many years," she told me. "He always blamed himself for your sins, though I hope you told him that you made your own choices."

"Yes, Mother, I did," I said. In a miracle I didn't understand, the anger I'd carried for so long was lifted. My father had done what he had done and I had done what I had done, and somehow we had both managed to find our place in the world and in God's grace. It was enough.

"He wants to talk to Nephi," I said.

"Then you will have to go get him," Mother said.

I looked at Naomi and saw the fierceness in her eyes. "You make him come," she told me. "Do not give him a choice. His father wants to see him one last time and his father deserves that much respect. That temple of his will have to come second for once."

I nodded to her and went out to the temple site.

Nephi wasn't anywhere to be seen and I worried for a moment that I would have to go out to wherever it was he quarried the stone. I didn't know if I had that much time—or if Father did.

But then I saw his head pop out behind one of the decorations he was carving on the outer stone and I waved and called to him. He was too preoccupied to hear me.

It took several minutes for me to reach him physically and when I did, he struck me reflexively. "Laman, I still have the power of God to smite you, if necessary. I am doing God's work here and—"

"Nephi, I'm not trying to stop your work. Father is dying and has asked for you to come to him one last time."

Nephi hesitated, looking around at the temple. "My work here is important. I am the only one God has trusted to do this."

"I know that, Nephi, but Father was God's trusted prophet. Perhaps he has some last precious words for you from God." It was the only thing I could think of to make Nephi listen to me and go to Father. Just their relationship alone did not seem to be enough.

Nephi wiped at his brow, and then bent down to pick up his chisel.

"Nephi, go now!" I said sharply, yanking the chisel from his hands. "I will work on this for you if that's what I must do to get you to go see our Father. It is his last wish." I didn't bother to tell Nephi anything that Father had told me about being sorry for treating Nephi and Sam better. It didn't matter anymore. It was past and gone.

"No, don't," said Nephi, pointing at the chisel.

At first I thought he was going to take it back and refuse me. Then I would have had to decide if I was willing to knock Nephi unconscious and take him to Father forcibly in that state. I was.

But Nephi said, "I don't trust you to do the decoration as it must be done."

I put the chisel down slowly. "You will go to see Father now?" I asked.

"I will go if you promise to leave the temple as it is," he said.

"I promise, then," I said. He had spent so many months trying to get me to help with the temple that I was surprised at his change of mind now. But perhaps he had only wanted me to do the hard labor, not the delicate work of the suns and moons on the temple face.

I watched as Nephi moved toward Father's home. He grew smaller and smaller and I wanted to shout at him all the accomplishments I had made, show him all the buildings I had finished around him, as he worked on his one, remind him that his own family owed me for their home. But I didn't.

The temple was magnificent. And I didn't know how to finish the decorations.

I left the chisel where it was and asked for young Lehi and young Nephi to come and guard the temple. I didn't know if that was truly necessary, but I didn't want to hear Nephi complain that something had happened to his work while he was gone. I didn't know how long it would be, but I told my sons that I would make sure they had food at mealtimes, and reminded them how much I had trusted them all their lives.

Nephi went in and Father spent many hours proclaiming blessings over him. He was told that he would see the temple finished and that it would be as it was meant to be. Also that his children would see Christ Himself when God chose to come down to His people in the meridian of time and show Himself to them. He was told that he would have many sons and daughters, though he had only one as of yet. And on and on, of the future when Nephi's name would be spoken by many for good. And that the words he had written on his own plates would be whispered through every country in every land in the world.

After Nephi, Lemuel and Sam and Jacob and Joseph came for blessings.

Lemuel was angry when he left. I could see it, but I didn't have time to ask him why. Had Father asked him for forgiveness, too, and Lemuel was not ready to give it?

I went in to see Father one last time, but he was already gone. I knelt at his side and wept and promised him that I would do as he had asked and make sure that the family stayed together even after he was gone. In that moment, I meant it. But I didn't understand how difficult it would become.

We buried Father the next day, though Nephi did none of the digging of the grave. He was too busy with the temple again and did not even come for the funeral.

Mother did not live long after Father. We buried her the next week, right next to Father's grave.

Nephi was busy with the temple. Of course he was. And what could be more important than that to any man?

29

Ten years later, things were much the same. Nephi was constantly working in the temple, though he never invited any of us to come into it and see what he was doing. He said that we had to go through a purification ritual to prove that we were worthy to enter the House of the Lord. He said that he would have to pray to God to have a confirmation that we belonged there with him. Needless to say, none of us bothered with that. We had plenty to do without entering his special temple, though he did very little to help the rest of us in our tasks.

I admired his attention to detail and his artistic integrity, but I was tired of him never paying attention to his family's needs and focusing on the temple alone.

It was when Nephi's wife went into labor and Nephi would not come out of the temple that Naomi began to speak out against him. What kind of father was he going to be, if he was never there for his own child? We would always have to do everything for him, she complained. He was a burden to the rest of us. We should declare him mad and turn his temple into an asylum.

I went up to talk to Nephi after that. I knocked on the door of the temple and declared myself. I had to wait a full hour before Nephi would come down and speak to me with the door open between us.

"How are you?" I asked.

He looked exhausted. He looked almost as old as Father had, when we had arrived here and he had been so close to death. Maybe we wouldn't have to do anything at all to rid ourselves of him.

But when he spoke, he sounded full of energy. "The temple will be glorious, Laman. We cannot do less for our God, who has saved our lives and brought us all here to this place of bounty. Our gratitude should be endless."

I put a hand on his shoulder. "Nephi, brother, we worry for you. You so rarely come out of the temple. I know it is holy work you do here, but your wife—your new son— they need you."

"God will protect them for me," said Nephi.

"Yes, I'm sure He will." Through the rest of us. We did not have anything against innocent children or against Nephi's poor wife. "But Nephi, don't you want to enjoy your child's early years? Think of what you are missing. All that time that Father spent with you when you were small. Don't you remember him carrying you around, showing you the world? Teaching you letters when you were too young to read? He did it because he loved you and wanted to make sure that you knew how much."

Father had done all that for Nephi that he had not done for me and Lemuel. It was strange to be in a position now to save Nephi's son from the fate that had been ours.

"I love him," said Nephi. "Of course I do. I went to see him last night, and his mother. They are well. They don't need me."

"They do need you, Nephi," I said. "You want your son to grow up to know God, don't you? How can that happen if you are not there to teach him?"

Nephi considered this for a long moment. To my astonishment, his eyes teared up and he nodded. "You're right,

Laman. You're a good brother. After all we have been through together, I know that you love me even still. Despite how many times I have had to correct you, for you to correct me shows that you are working to become a better man."

He came out of the temple then, and I thought that I might still manage to do what Father had asked of me on his deathbed, to keep the family together.

Nephi spent weeks outside of the temple and with his family. For the first time, Naomi did not have to make sure that his wife and child had food to eat and she began to say kind things about him, for he was an attentive, loving father to his children when he was with them.

But it lasted only a year and then Nephi went back to the temple, bringing his son with him, though he was still too young to walk or speak. Nephi brought the child out to nurse from his mother, then took him back inside. I tried to tell myself that at least he was spending time with his son, but Nephi's wife was melancholy. She wept constantly and Naomi began to complain about Nephi again.

"You should be ashamed to have him as your brother," she said.

"He has good and bad in him, like the rest of us. And I truly believe that he speaks to God." Though he had given us no new direction in quite some time. What did we need? We were already in the place where we were meant to be.

"I don't care who he speaks to. I care if he acts the part of a man in our community. He must spend time in the fields, and on the hunt. He must raise his son with the other boys," she said. "If he doesn't, I have a mind to burn down that temple of his and make him give it up."

The temple was mostly stone, but there were wooden parts of it, and even stone could be damaged by fire, not to mention Nephi himself.

"Let me talk to him again," I said.

She agreed to give me a day before she carried out her plan.

I went to the temple. "I fear for you, Nephi. I do not mean to frighten you, but there are many in the family who are angry with you."

"The wicked are always angry at the words of the righteous," said Nephi. It was a variation on what I had heard him say many times before, in Jerusalem, in the wilderness, on the ship. He saw everything in terms of black and white, and he was always the one who was free of sin.

But I had promised Father. "I'm not talking about righteousness, Nephi. I'm talking about sharing in the work of the community. Working in the fields, hunting, preparing food. People see you in the temple every day and you do none of that." Why would he not hear me?

"I am doing the work that matters most. God has commanded it, and our people need it in the future. Where will we go to show our devotion to God if this is not finished? Where will the new prophet come to receive dreams and visions of God? Where will Christ appear when he is born and dies and comes to preach to our descendants as I have seen in vision?"

"Nephi, you and Father received dreams and visions without a temple," I pointed out. "Why can't the future generations do the same?" Why couldn't Christ come to teach our children's children without a temple?

"You don't understand. This is to show God that we recognize His hand in saving us. We would not be here in this Promised Land without His help. We can never let our children forget that," said Nephi.

"I know that, but can you work on the temple part days instead of all day? Can you help in the planting and harvesting at all? You do not understand how angry certain people are with you." I was trying to help my brother, but he wasn't listening to me.

"God will protect me," said Nephi, looking into the clear skies and the bright sun in them. "And until the temple is finished, I can do no other work."

"Nephi, listen to me. You cannot expect God to send an angel down every time you offend someone else. We are here in the Promised Land now. It is time for you to rejoin us, to act as if you are one of us instead of above us." I had not come angry, but I could feel the emotion swelling in my heart. Father had said that Nephi shouldn't be above us. Why didn't he see that it was true?

"But we're not meant to be always grubbing for food. We are meant to be above the ordinary concerns. Isn't that why God brought us to this place? There is food on trees, ready to be picked. We need do very little to keep ourselves alive. And we can devote ourselves fully to God."

How could he say such stupid things? "You can do that because the rest of us labor for you and your family! We do not merely pick fruit from trees, Nephi. We plant and water and weed and harvest. God doesn't simply give us a living. We have to work for it. Can't you see that?"

Apparently not, for his eyes glazed over and he closed the wooden door to the temple on me.

A wooden door that would burn, I thought.

I should have pushed away the evil thought, but I was so angry that it festered in my mind until I had built a fire at the door of the temple and blew on it until it caught and began to lick at the wood. Nephi didn't notice what I had done until it was too late. He was too busy on his own work.

I justified myself by saying that Nephi had said that God would protect him. Let this be the proof to him that it was not so, that he could not always rely on an angel coming down to save him.

Indeed, no angel came to blow out the flames. No rainstorm darkened the sky above the temple. The thick door caught fire, and then the smoke rose both within and without the temple.

I could hear Nephi coughing and choking inside. I could hear him scramble to the top of the temple, his son slung over his back. I felt a moment of shame that I had done this, to a baby.

And then the shame was gone and all I felt was satisfaction that my plan had worked, that Nephi would at last come out of his temple and that he would never be able to go back inside it, for the flames were eating all his work, and they were darkening the beautiful white stones on the outside. This would never be fit to be a house of God.

Nephi called out through one of the top windows for help. I laughed at him and told him to throw the baby down to me. I would have caught him. I was angry, but not at the child.

Nephi refused. He didn't trust me, for some reason. He called me a child of Satan, and said that I would never be able to repent of this wrong, that God would punish me and my children for all eternity.

I walked away at that and would have let both him and the babe burn to death.

But Sam and Jacob and Joseph heard him and went to him. They caught the babe in a blanket, and then coaxed

Nephi into jumping, as well. I heard the cry of triumph when he stepped out of the blanket, safe, but for a few burns on his face and arms.

I could have gone to him then and told him I was sorry. I could have bent on my knees and asked for forgiveness. The anger was already fading, and I knew that I had been wrong. I had been a child of Satan, and I didn't want my children to be cursed, even if I knew that I believed no mercy—from either Nephi or God. But I was too proud to do it.

And so in the morning, they were all gone.

Nephi, his wife, and son.

Sam, and his whole family.

Jacob and Joseph and their families.

The clearing where we had built so many homes and where we had become a family again in truth, after Father's death, was quiet with accusation against me. My sons asked me where their friends had gone. Young Lehi had been about to marry a daughter of Jacob. She was gone without a trace. She had sent no message to him. He was heartbroken, and he blamed me.

Of course he blamed me. It was all my fault.

Naomi had planned to burn the temple, but I had done it.

I was the most wretched of men. I had let Father down, and God, as well. Our family was now forever sundered, because of my evil.

I'd believed I had grown wiser and kinder and more faithful, but it was all a lie. I was the same man I had been in the wilderness when I had fled into the sandstorm, when I had beaten Nephi with a staff, when I'd helped tie Nephi to the ship.

Nephi had cursed my children through me and I could never undo that. I would have to live with the knowledge of my mistakes through the rest of my life. And through eternity, if Nephi was right, and there was an after-life where I would continue to be the man I was now. I would continue to feel this weight of pain on my chest, this fire everywhere through my body, this poison in my veins.

I wished I had never been born. I wished that my mother had strangled me at birth. I wished that I had died of starvation in those years when Father had left us. I wished that the angel who had been sent to us before had killed me a touch. Or that Nephi had, when he had warned me that he had the power of God in him.

Why wasn't I the one who was thrown overboard instead of the son of Ishmael? He would have been a better man than I was. He would not have caused this split in our family.

We searched for them. Oh, how we searched. To no avail. They were gone into the jungle and I did not know if they had gone south or north. My sons and I traveled for many days, but there was no sign of them.

30

It has been many years now since Nephi and the others left us. We have continued to grow and the homes that were once deserted are now filled, along with many others. We have planted the fields with all the seeds that the daughters of Ishmael brought with them. Nephi and his people did not take any of those with them, though I would gladly have given half to be fair. His wife and the wives of the others were also daughters of Ishmael, and entitled to a portion of his inheritance for them.

Lemuel and I are not friends, let alone as close as brothers should be. I have rebuilt the temple in penance for what I did to Nephi and to his young son, and for what I did to the temple itself. I scrubbed the outside stones until they were pure white again. And inside, I did all that I could to remake Nephi's decorations, though some were so badly damaged that I could not do anything more than guess at what Nephi meant. I do not understand the signs and symbols on them, and I have never asked God to reveal them to me.

In fact, I have never prayed again since Nephi left. How could I? I could only ask God to take my life, and that seemed a cruel thing to do to my wife and my children. And so I remain as I am, outcast and tainted by sin. I will die in my sin, as Nephi warned me, and I will never be able to repent.

But at least the temple is here. Once I finished it, I closed the door which I remade as close to possible as Nephi's door, and I locked it. It is waiting here for Nephi to return to, or his sons or grandsons. We are not worthy to dedicate such a place ourselves, but it remains a reminder of what we have lost, and what we wish to gain back.

Lemuel tells stories about how arrogant and grasping Nephi was, that he was always eager to be above us in all things. I do not say that he is wrong. He tells the details right, sometimes mimicking Nephi's voice perfectly enough to make me laugh. And yet, he misses the whole of the story, the meat of it.

We were the ones who were selfish and above ourselves. We are the ones filled with evil who would not listen when truth was spoken to us, however hard it was.

And we are paying the price of that.

The Promised Land no longer produces its fruit so easily. The animals have become feral and difficult to hunt. And we see the natural consequences of our own small minds and dark hearts in our children, who fight regularly.

There was a murder two years ago. It was Lemuel's son, found on the ground with his throat cut. No one admitted to the deed, and in retaliation, Lemuel killed one of my sons. I tried to speak to my other sons to stop the bloodshed, but they would not heed me. And so Lemuel also left our community, taking all his people with him. They swore vengeance against me and mine, swore that they would kill us all, one by one. And so they have done.

One death here, one body there. I cannot stop my sons from doing the same in turn. We are engaged in a war already, and there are so few of us. We were supposed to have fled Jerusalem to avoid destruction and death, to avoid becoming slaves. But here we are slaves again, to anger and hatred.

I can blame no one but myself.

I am close to death now. I can feel it with every breath I take. It is a heavy weight in some ways, but in others, it will be such a relief. I welcome it as if it were Naomi come back to me, Naomi who died many years ago, though she was the one who deserved to live. An animal killed her when she was out in the field. An animal that should have been tame and harmless.

Last night I prayed.

It was the first time I have prayed in many years, and I felt a fool doing it. There was no reason to believe that God would hear me now, after I have compiled many other sins upon my gravest ones. But I did not pray for forgiveness that I thought a just God could never grant me. What I prayed for was my sons. I prayed that they would have another chance, that their children would one day be able to return to Nephi's people, that the temple would be dedicated and used again.

And God granted me a vision. At last.

I could scarce believe it when it came, for I knew I did not deserve it. Had I become a visionary man at last, as my father and brother were before me?

I saw my children and Nephi's children and they were standing together by a building that looked very much like the temple Nephi had first built for us. Could it be the same one that Nephi had seen when he had begun building? Had he built a new one in the new land where he had gone?

And coming out of the heavens was Christ Himself. I knew Him because He was suffused in light and surrounded by angels who were calling out his name and singing. The group of people on the ground knelt and hid their heads from Him until He called to them to come to Him and He blessed them all.

I wept as I saw this, that my descendants would one day see Christ and know Him, that they would be worthy to worship Him freely, as I am not.

And then a voice came to me and said, "Laman, you are forgiven. Your children will one day call you blessed, that you brought them to this new land. Nephi's children and your children will together create a world of peace. They will write their own scriptures and honor the Brass Plates which you sacrificed so much to bring with you to them. They will remember you, and the lessons that you have taught them. And they will know that no one is ever too far from God to repent."

I woke from the dream and felt as if I were a young man once more. I wanted to dance and kiss everyone I met, but when I tried to stand up, I felt my age come upon me once more. I told my sons about the vision I had had, with Christ standing in the midst of their children one day, and with Nephi's. They laughed at me and told me that I was getting old and that my dreams were a fantasy of a dying mind.

I thought of how Lemuel and I had laughed at my father and I felt satisfied that I was experiencing all of the parts of being a visionary man. I was a fool, and I did not care. I knew my dream did not make sense. There was no reason to believe that it would happen, since Nephi and his people had been lost to us for many years. And yet I wanted it to be true.

I prayed again this morning, and thanked God for His goodness to me in all things, through all times, through the good and the bad. I will pray every day from now until my dying day, and I will write my record upon plates that I make with my own hands, as Nephi wrote on his plates— new scriptures for a new day. Perhaps my record will be destroyed when I am dead. Perhaps my children will see no value in it, for I have not taught them well to see the hand of God in their lives. It does not matter to me. God will do what He deems right, for me and my people. That is all that I can hope for, and I praise His name forever more.

END

Afterword

I lost faith in God completely in 2007 after the still-birth of my sixth child and spent the next five years as an atheist. In 2012, I decided that I wanted to try to believe again. I'd felt very alone, in a spiritual way, despite the fact that I'd continued to attend the Mormon ward in my neighborhood. And so began a full year of me trying to pray to God and ending up saying the only thing I found I could say with real conviction, which was, "I don't believe in you." I said it over and over again, night after night, because I was determined not to fall back on the old platitudes that I'd once used and that had ended up failing me. And then, one night, I prayed more than that. And a little more. And the journey had truly begun.

Writing my Linda Wallheim mysteries has been part of my journey back to Mormonism, a way to try to make a model of a Mormon woman I might someday be able to become. It hasn't been entirely successful. Linda is a compilation of some of the amazing, faithful Mormon women I knew and admired (women like Sue Gong, Jody England Hansen, Neca Allgood, Debra Coe, and Lisa Glad). She isn't me, though I've often wished she were. I'm still clinging on to faith by the skin of my teeth most of the time. But there are bursts of brilliance that strike me now and again and convince me that there's value in the struggle. And maybe, just maybe, there's a place for me in Mormonism.

As I returned to The Book of Mormon as someone whose faith had been crushed and was still fragile, I found myself uninspired by the Nephi in its pages. In my youth, I'd been determined to be that Nephi, always stalwart, always sure of himself and of his revelations from God. But that wasn't me anymore and sometimes I wanted to shake him. Couldn't he see hard what he was asking was? Couldn't he just once see things from the perspective of his less faithful, less valiant brothers who were just human beings? I'm far more Laman and Lemuel these days than I am Nephi. Does that mean that I'm doomed to hell? If that's true, why am I trying so hard?

And so the idea for this book was born, which I promptly dropped everything to write in a very busy October of 2014. I had no idea that it would ever be published. I didn't write it for anyone but myself, really. I didn't trust the Mormon publishers currently on the scene to do justice to the story, and I'd tried self-publishing without much success. It was just my attempt to tell the story of someone who was deeply flawed but still trying to grapple with the divine, and who also deserved, in my opinion, to have a story told.

Many people helped me tell this story. Candice Stevens, Jeffrey Creer, Quinn Colter, Kevin Cummings, and Erin Jensen for looking at the earliest version of this book. You'll see changes here that have made it stronger and that is because of your careful concern.

What I hope now, as I send this out into the world, is that there are other readers out there who need to see Laman's story because it's theirs, too. He's redeemed in the end, not because he deserves it for his faithfulness, but because God's love is infinite and encompasses even the wicked brothers. God never forgets them. He never gives up on them. And that, ultimately, is why I've returned to faith, and to Mormonism.

Mette Harrison

Mette Ivie Harrison is a former scripture chase champion and Benson scholar. She is the author of multiple award-winning YA novels including *The Princess and the Hound,* as well as the national bestselling mystery series beginning with *The Bishop's Wife.* She holds a PhD in Germanic Languages and Literatures from Princeton University and is an All-American triathlete and multiple Ironman finisher. She lives with her husband and various of her five children in Layton, Utah.

72106048R00143

Made in the USA
Lexington, KY
28 November 2017